Mythical

Louisa Barnes

Contents

Chapter 1- History

I place my head on the cold glass, my wavy brown hair falling over my eyes. How could they? How could my family do that to me?

I sigh, remembering that year.

------Flashback------

"What do you mean, mom?" I snarl at my step-mother.

"I-I, um, y-you a-are...." My step-mother stammers, frightened like a doe. "We are sending you to Mythical School...." My father says simply.

I growl, "You mean you are selling me to mythical school!"

My 'father' looks at me, emotionless, "Why do you think that?"

"You are so afraid of me transforming into something more powerful than you that you are selling me away! You knew mom's animal, and knew she was powerful, that's why you let her die!" I scream in tears.

My father growls, and turns around. "Take her away," he whispers dangerously.

I scream, shout, and kick as my father's strong men grab my arms and drag me out of the room. "You are so low that you have to sell me to get money!" I holler out, not even getting a reaction from my father.

A guard quickly slaps his rough hand over my mouth. I yell into his hand but no sound comes out.

My older half-sister sneers, "Have fun at 'school'. Too bad you can't transf orm.... Then maybe you would be special." My sister took my dad's side of transforming into a werewolf. It is rare for a female to be able to transform so my sister likes to rub it into peoples' faces.

I growl, my eyes flashing from their normal hazelnut brown color to electric blue. I smirk as my sister, Sheila, steps back in surprise. The anger returns.

The guards keep pulling me out. I quickly skim over my 'family'. My father was disappointed, my step-mother in fear, and Sheila in shock. I growl, such a nice family. (Sarcasm)

"Sissy?" A small voice whispers, creeping from the doorway. I give a small smile to my younger half-brother, "Hey bro..."

Clear sorrow was plastered on his young little face. I look at him and sigh. He looks so much like mom, "Take care of yourself, for me, please?" I ask.

William, his brown eyes glossy and his hair messy, nods, "Come home soon, Kathy." I whisper as I feel the painful sleeping shot puncture my skin, "I will....."

-----Flashback ends----- That was 5 years ago. I am 17 now.

The 'school', it turns out, was actually more of a prison. They did things to kids to make them forget that they have the power to transform into a mythical creature. They even tried on me, but ha, how wrong they were to do that.

I transformed 5 years earlier than normal, on the night of my mother's death. Nobody knew, and I made sure to keep it that way. I learned to mask the scent. However, on the night I transformed, at age 10, I learned my creature is extremely strong. I don't remember what animal I am for I was to grief stricken to remember.

But I was scared of my creature's power.

After a while in this school, however, I decided to run out. So, one random night in the 'prison', I decided it was time to break free from its torturous walls. I escaped and quickly became a free-runner. Free-runners are outcast Mythical Creatures. They usually don't have a pack/family and have difficulty surviving in the Mythical World.

I smile remembering my last fight. Free-Runner females are very rare. Free-runner transformer females were even rarer. Many people try to take advantage of Free-Runner females because they usually can't defend themselves. But boy, people quickly learned their mistake when they try to mess with me. Yes, I do get into fights a lot.

But to tell you the truth, I like my life; just being an outcast. However, all Free-Runner who have been reported strong were quickly taken and shoved on a bus where they learned they are going to Mythical Academy. Mythical Academy holds some of the strongest creatures, so they decided to give Free-Runners a chance to prove themselves to be worthy and powerful. This sucks because I apparently was reported multiple times.

"Alright gentlemen," the intercom of the bus sounds. I cough angrily. "Oh and lady, we will be arriving to the Academy in 5 minutes so get yourselves and your stuff ready to be boarded off."

I sigh, taking out my headphones and putting them into my backpack. Forget the past. My eyes gaze the landscape outside. It was a rainy day. However the gorgeous forest with mountains behind the sea of trees was still seen. The forest slowly blends into a beach that had white shores and peaceful waters. The gray overcast adds a calm but dark mood to the landscape. This was a perfect place for all creatures; apparently.

The bus stops rapidly. I hiss as I slam into the seat in front of me. "Hey! Watch it!" yells a male voice from up ahead of me.

I mumble a quick 'sorry' and look down.

The boy pops out from behind the seat. He had well-groomed raven black hair with aqua blue eyes. His jawline was sharp and strong. His body was well-defined with muscles and his posture just screamed power. He had a nice complexion of olive skin and was gorgeously fit. I would be drooling if my years as a free-runner didn't teach me otherwise. "Hey, look at me when you talk to me, slut-runner" he sneers.

*B*tch mode activated* I look up at the cocky boy as things click. I realize he is probably the student who was assigned to this bus to make sure we don't start a fight.

A slut-runner is usually the name for Free-runner females. This name came around for a way to survive as a free-runner female is to have fun with men in bed; therefore, the name slut.

"Say that again pretty boy!" I snarl. He raises an eyebrow, amused, "What are you going to do slut-runner? Make me pay? How much you charge?" He smirks.

I growl, knowing that if I step out of line I will be severely punished. This isn't the streets, this is a much nicer community; apparently. He sneers, his eyes flashing red.

I allow my eyes to flicker blue then back brown. I grin as he jolts slightly.

"We are here, please exit the bus, and good luck this school year!" The intercom sounds.

I quickly stand up, heaving my backpack across one shoulder, and leaving the shocked boy in his seat.

There were hundreds of students on the large grass field in front of the school. The school was a small one story building. It had a simple tan coloring and was quite small. Most classes were outside in the huge empty grass field that surrounded the school.

Almost all the normal mythical creatures were looking at the buses that were unloading free-runners hatefully. Though, a few surprised looks were shot my way as I step out of the bus. I look around, already hating this year.

I feel a breath on my shoulder and goosebumps run down my arms, "You should not have made that move, free-runner."

Chapter 2- New People

I sigh, turning around to the boy. At least it isn't slut-runner anymore. I glare at him, "What do you want?"

He grins in a cocky matter, "You have an interesting fire free-runner. But, I want your name."

I narrow my eyes, "Why?"

"I'll tell you mine....."

I stiffen as I see shadows move closer to me; of course he has to bring his friends. "No, you will force me, based on the group of people coming our way," I say tilting my head toward where his friends were. They were a good enough distance enough to seem that they weren't eavesdropping, but their eyes tell another story.

The boy tilts his own head, taking in my keen awareness of the environment and people within it. He smirks in a roguish way, "I'm Ethan, what's your name?

I hesitate.

"Well?"

I sigh, "Kate. Now if you excuse me, I have elsewhere to be then in a kill circle." I quickly stalk past Ethan noticing the surprised looks on his friends' faces. Most free-runner females want to be back in a pack/family so they were always hitting on guys. Ha, not me.

I shake my head, hating this more and more every second. I storm into the small looking high school, students moving away as I pass by. Quickly, I grab my schedule from the front desk and skim through it.

~~

ScienceFightingMath Lunch HistoryEnglishGymMagic

~~~

Oooh. Fighting actually sounds fun. I could use a good fight right about now. I sigh as I shove my schedule into my pocket and storm to my first classroom.

Nobody was here yet so I got the choice of seating. I quickly grab a seat towards the back of classroom, closest to the window. I place in my head-phones and allow the time to pass.

Time ticks as everybody trickles in and class begins. My teacher was a man who was looking in his 50's. He was old, and seemed like he didn't care anymore. He literally said: "Do whatever you want, we will start tomorrow. Oh here are the rules." That's all we did. Got a page with the rules and then he slept the rest of the class. So, I allowed my gaze to travel to the window, just taking in the mountains and the sea of trees.

A sharp pain cuts across my cheek. In reflex, I spin around in my chair towards the source. I find a group of guys laughing. And who was in the middle? Ethan, of course.
~~~

I feel the hot blood leak down my cheek. I quickly wipe it up, hiding the wound in hope that nobody notices how fast I heal. I feel the familiar warmth and know that my cut was gone. I turn back towards the front and plop back into my chair, trying to ignore their taunts. My music gets louder in my ears. Just ignore them. I take the pencil that cut me and examine it.

A perfectly good pencil, why use it on me? I grit my teeth. "Because they think I am weak," I think to myself. I sigh, just fiddling with the pencil, ignoring the cat-calls they were sending my way.

"SPLASH!" A wave of water hit me. I gasp, freezing in shock as I got soaked to the bone; and it was freezing!!! A wave of laughter explodes in the room. My jaw drops down. I pull out my head phones, my mouth still unhinged. Flicking my hands to get rid of the water, I look around to find my prankster.

The son of Poseidon, Jack, was levitating a ball of water while laughing his head off. Jack is one of the most crushed on guys. Every girl wanted to be with him, even those not in this school. Why am I not surprised he is in that little 'group'?

I take a deep controlled breath, and look at my soaked clothing. "SPLASH!" "SNAP!" I feel the pencil snap in two in my hand as the second ball of water falls on my head.

This only caused a louder laughing session to begin. I growl, "I can't take this." I stand up, getting the boys attention and look at them. "You just messed with the wrong runner...." I snarl.

"Ooo, I'm so scared" laughs Jack, his blue eyes shining with mischief. He flicks his white blonde hair away as I grab my backpack, swinging it over my shoulder and storm out of the classroom.

"Where you going, babe?" sneers another boy.

I give a fake smile, knowing that I should be 'nice' to higher class students, "The bell rang...Honey," I hiss the last word and turn on my heal.

God they are so stupid! "Let us escort you to your next class then, sugar." smirks a familiar voice. I exhale deeply, allowing my tongue to run circles in my mouth as I try to control my anger.

"I'll pass...." I say through gritted teeth and squeak out of the classroom.

Ethan snatches my schedule out of my hand. "Hey!" I yell turning on my heal to face him. "Give it back!" I growl trying to snatch it back.

I gasp as his hand grabs mine, causing my skin to catch fire with tingles. Warmth blooms in my stomach. He smirks at my reaction then responds, "Looks like you have your next class with me....May I escort you now?"

I pull my hand back, hugging my shivering body. "F-f-fine..." I chatter as I glare at this cocky boy. "Come on then!" A fourth boy says, throwing his hand over my shaking shoulders. I looked up at him in shock while he just grins, his brown eyes sparkling. "Relax, I don't bite," He smirks, brushing away some of his hazel hair from his eyes.

"But I do..." I think to myself. "By the way, I'm Will, that's Jack, he's Ethan, and he is Léo." The chocolate eyed boy continues. My eyes travel to where Will's finger points. There stood a gorgeous lion. His mane was sleek black, tan fur, and piercing emerald green eyes. I step back in horror. This school has wild zoo animals running around in it?!

I feel my mouth fall open, again. This lion was twice the size of a normal lion! He looked like a horse! The lion quickly transforms into a handsome boy. Black hair, tan skin, and emerald eyes. His eyes flashed and quickly changed to grey. I blink, his eyes change like mine! He's an animal transformer! I didn't know they had animal transformers in Mythical Academy... Perhaps I may fit in?

He walks over, throwing me a crooked smile, "Hello, what might your name be?" I look him over intently, wondering if I should tell him.

"Her name is Kate." Ethan replies for me. He throws me a smirk while I feel myself grind my teeth. Perhaps not.

"RING!" sounds the bell. "Come on guys, don't want the free-runner to be late on her first day now do we?" Jack says, playing with some of the rain water.

I begin to shiver more as Will pushes me to the raining outside to get to fighting class.

Chapter 3- Fights

"Hello class!" grins the young teacher. She was a beautiful female, probably in her late 30s with blonde hair and sharp grey eyes.

She turns around, looking at all the students in the circle around her, "Today, we are going to see what level each of you are and place you with the class you belong. There are four statuses. We have Outcast status, which is the lowest one and where you know no fighting. The next level is the Free-runners where you know some basic fighting moves and techniques. Then we have Normals where you do fighting but are not advanced or had no real fighting experiences. Finally, we have the highest class, Pureblood. If you make it here it means you can beat or equal our best fighters. You must have speed, strength, experience, and know more advanced fighting moves."

She flashes us a smile, showing her sharp teeth, "We begin fights in 10 minutes!" She snaps her fingers making everything disappear.

I land with my face slamming into the hard floor. A hiss of pain erupting from the back of my throat. "Ooh, you must be that free-runner girl! Sorry for not warning you!" A high pitched voice says worriedly.

I push myself up from the tiled floor and notice that I have been teleported into a locker room. I rub my forehead, looking around the area. To my left showers and bathrooms. To my right a long row of lockers with two lockers on each stack. My eyes finally travel to the girl in front of me.

She gives me a small smile, "Forgive me?" "Wait what? Oh Ya! Sure I guess ..." I respond, mumbling, still lost trying to figure out how Ms. Fangtooth, the teacher, teleported us.

The girl goes into a full-blown smile, flicking her golden brown hair away from her eyes. Her caramel eyes shine as she holds out her hand, "I'm Anna. I'm an animal transformer!"

I smile, I already like this girl, she doesn't seem to care that I am a free-runner, "I'm Kate. I'm not really sure what I am..."

Lies. I'm an animal transformer too.

Anna smiles, "Well you don't have to worry about the fight. They put all new free-runners with easy people so you won't get hurt."

I raise my eyebrow at her. She grins, "I'm guessing you don't want easy?" I smile back, "You got me." We both burst into laughter. After catching our breaths, Anna leads me to my locker; which, conveniently, was right next to hers.

I pull out a pair of grey capris sweatpants with an orange phoenix logo on the bottom and a black tank-top. "Are these mine?" I ask Anna. She nods her head, smiling, "All of our clothes and supplies are gotten for us before we arrive.

"Ah," I quickly slip off my soaking clothing and put on the tank-top and sweatpants.

"Oh! Make sure to tie up your hair in a ponytail! Ms. Fangtooth is very picky about that on the first day." Anna quickly pipes up as she finishes tying her sneakers.

I roll my eyes; I hate having my hair up when it comes to fighting, people can use the ponytail against you. Long hair too, but mythical creature fighting? A ponytail is easier to pin-point with magic. But I did what I was told.

Hooking my arm up with hers, Anna takes me through the locker room and to the fighting room.

My mouth drops and a slight smile reaches my lips. The place was amazing! It was at least two stories in height with hanging ropes, steam beams, slabs of wood, pipes, and anything else you can think be hanging. Right smack in the middle was an area with a cushioned floor. Around the arena lay all sorts of weapons and other tools.

"This is amazing!" I squeal lightly, noticing how the room's outer wall could open like a garage door to show the outside field. Anna laughs, "I'm guessing you like fighting?"

I nod, grinning.

Anna grins back, "Come on then, let's warm up." She quickly takes me to a corner of the room where we go through warm-ups and talk a little about ourselves. Anna, turns out, can transform into a leopard. Léo was her mate. I quickly learned a little about her pack. Which for me, was hell, for the pack was Ethan's little group. It turns out Ethan's pack was the pack in control of this territory, and I already managed to rile them up.

"So ya, Léo is a lion and is my mate. Jack is a demigod. Will is a wolf transformer, though not a werewolf. His mate is a girl named Linda and she is a fairy. Jack and Ethan are single Pringles." giggles Anna.

I smile taking a drink from my water bottle. "We have two single girls living with us. We have Athena; daughter of Athena. It's really weird. We also have Sheila, a werewolf transformer."

I choke on my water as I heard Sheila's name, "S-Sheila?" I cough, my eyes as large as saucers.

Anna nods, patting me on my back, "Ya, she lives in our pack house, and is hitting badly on Ethan. She thinks she is his mate." "And annoying she is....." I hear a deep voice complain.

I turn around to find Ethan standing there. My eyes travel down his form, sweatpants and a tank-top like me, but he looks so muscular. His arms were rippling with muscles, showing health and physical fitness. Yum.

He smirks, "You done?" I shake my head, my cheeks flushing at being caught.

Anna giggles, giving Ethan a hug, "Hey there, pack-daddy." Ethan groans, "I told you not to call me that!"

Anna replies smugly, "Then don't tease my friend!" Anna winks at me as I look at her in surprise; she called me her friend? That was fast....

The rest of boys quickly pile in laughing and tossing about. Jack flashes me a smile, "Ready to go down, runner?"

"What?" I ask, confused. "You are fighting me first, so better get ready if you want revenge on me..." winks Jack.

Perfect.

I look over to Anna, "I thought you said free-runners get easy people...." "Well....." starts Anna.

"AMANDA HOWL AND GABSON FROST! You are up first!" shouts Ms. Fangtooth as the final students pile in.

I sigh, walking over to the cushioned fighting arena, and beginning to watch the fights.

-------Some time later-------- I sigh, bored. Almost everyone here was either in the group of free-runner or outcast. It was boring to watch. But hey, being a free-runner meant you got to watch a lot of interesting fights that usually didn't end with an 'I yield!'. "Ms. Scalewing and Jack Poseidon! You are up!"

"Good luck!" smiles Anna.

I smile back and make my way to the fighting floor to take my stand across from Jack. My features were back to the hard-cold that they were used too.

He smirks, looking me up and down and raising his fists in warning.What a child. "3, 2, 1, GO!" shouts Ms. Fangtooth as me and Jack just watch each other.

My brain starts to whirl. Okay, he is weaker on his left side. He won't be able to throw me off then. However, he has water magic. That is problematic. If I pin him down, that should do it. He is also very proud, let's use that against him.

I duck quickly as the first water ball shoots at my head, aiming at my ponytail. I realize he is trying to hit me in my face by using my hair. I coyly grin, my hand quickly undoing my ponytail. My hair cascades down to my shoulders as I toy, "Come on, you can do better."

Jack raises an eyebrow, "Want to go tough, huh runner?" I snarl happily, "Bring it!"

He attacks head on and I grin. Ducking under his arm, I grab his left hand, and flip him using it.

"Ugh!" He groans as his back smashes into the floor. I yelp as he grabs my foot, bringing me down. I twist my body, his hand leaving my ankle and allowing me to land on my hands. He stands.

I roll over as another water ball aims at me. Missed it! Jumping on my feet, I throw a punch to Jack's perfect face. He catches my fist with a grin. I grin back. Flicking my wrist I manage to slip my wrist out of his grasp, and grab his arm.

I smirk as his eyebrows shoot up in confusion. I pull him toward me, lacing my ankle in front of his, and tripping him. He yelps as he tilts forward. My hand travels to his shoulder, pushing downward. My other arm shoots under his belly and he flips around my arm. His back collides with the floor with a satisfying 'SMACK'. He moans loudly. I lean over him, grabbing him arms and holding them above his head as my knees keeps his pelvis down. Jack squirms, a full-blown smirk on his face as I apply more pressure to keep him down.

"3,2,1 stop!" Ms. Fangtooth shouts. I lift myself off of Jack, helping him up. "Good fight, runner, and I loved that's position by the way. I would love to try it again," He winks, leaving the arena as students clap around us. I roll my eyes, also exiting.

A few more couples fought as I stood at the side to see if I will be allowed to test for the pure blood class.

"Alright! Here are the results! Blah blah blah blah blah blah ect. Katherine Scalewing: normal! Blah blah blah blah." My eye bulge when she says I am in normal. Nobody was accepted into Pureblood! I feel my blood pressure rise and I grit my teeth. Ethan catches my eyes and smirks.

That does it for me, "Excuse me!" I shout out, catching my teacher's attention. "What is it Katherine?" She asks, annoyed.

"I would like to know the reason I am not in the Pureblood class." "Easy. You are a free-runner and have not proven yourself."

I raise my head slightly, "Then I would like a challenge." Ms. Fangtooth raises a doubtful eyebrow, "A challenge? It's not like you can get any higher."

I smugly counter back, "You said that if you equal or beat a Pureblood that you are worthy to be in that class. I want a fight with a pure blood." The class goes into 'ooo' and whispers explode around me.

Ms. Fangtooth smiles, crossing her arms. Her fingers thrum a steady beat on her arm, "You do know that I get to choose your challenger then?"

I nod my head, "Understood." "Fine, you get a fight against the strongest in the class. Prince Ethan? Will you please come up?"

I gulp, throwing my hair back into a ponytail and sighing. Let's do this!

Chapter 4- Test

"**B**REAK TIME!" Shouts Ms. Fangtooth as I pin Ethan under me.

Of course, she can't show that her strongest student is beaten by a free-runner!

Ethan smirks at my out-of-breath state, "You've got delicious blood, runner." He slowly licks his lip of my blood in a seductive, challenging matter.

I glare at him, still trying to catch my breath, "We can't. All. Be vampires. Who don't. Need. To breathe...."

Cocky vampire.

His smirk deepens as I stand up. My hand grabs my neck where the fang bite was. Yes, Ethan decided to bite me, as if we were toddlers! The familiar warmth spreads through my neck and travels through my body to heal all my cuts and bruises. I moan and roll my neck. The fang scars, however, don't heal. Sighing, I hop off the cushioned arena and over to Anna.

"OMG! OMG! OMG! You actually fought well! Though probably won't survive the next round, but still!" shrieks Anna.

I smile, walking over to her, "I hope the students enjoyed the good fight." She giggled, "You actually passed the secret test...." "What?" I ask, looking closely at her.

She quickly blushes and turns away. "Anna, I'm still waiting." I say in a sing-song-y voice. "Okay! Okay! I'll tell you," she whispers, and then giggles, "The secret test was to see who would stand up against the teacher to fight for the pureblood position. Purebloods always stand up for what's right. And you did! Even against bad odds. This last part was to see if you had enough fighting ability to match one of us. Which you did, but the next part ----"

"Anna!" Shouts Ethan. She instantly blushes, "I can't tell you more." A deep voice smirks from behind me, "Careful Anna, don't want to ruin the surprise for our little runner here."

I freeze as Ethan's warm fingers gently travel my neck and stop at where he bit me. My heart speeds up slightly as his warm fingers drum against the mark. A heat washes over me from the broad chest of the person behind me.

Ethan's lips touch his bite. His tongue quickly makes a dash out, touching my skin and the mark. The warm wetness sparks butterflies in my stomach. I shiver, feeling my heart speed up even more. "No! Stop it heart!" I mentally scream at myself. Ethan chuckles darkly, pulling away, "I don't think your heart can stop even if it wanted to."

I turn to face him, my eyes scanning his face for any sign of clues. I catch his brilliant blue eyes and gasp.

"You are reading my mind!" I scream inside my head. Ethan replies smugly, "Very good, runner. But please, lower your voice" I mentally cuss, looking away.

"Tut tut tut, you shouldn't cuss Runner, it's disrespectful." I glare at Ethan, crossing my arms. "If it's so disrespectful, then why are you still listening!?" I mentally respond. Ethan grins as Ms. Fangtooth shouts, "Back onto the fighting floor, you two!"

Taking my position onto the floor I begin my evaluations of Ethan again. His weight is too much to one side, I could use that.

Ethan shifts, his weight now equal on both feet.

"Have you forgotten something?" Ethan asks, his deep voice echoing in my head. I picture him mentally smirking though on the outside, he was acting serious. "Get out!" I shout back, noticing how my evaluation ideas have just been destroyed.

The whistle blows and he attacks. I dodge to my left, missing his fist by an inch. He grins, "My turn runner."

In less than an eye blink, I am somehow pinned under him. He holds my hands above my head and his blue eyes hold mine. I forget how to breathe for a second.

God, he was sooooo good looking. Ew what?! You are fighting, you idiot!

Ethan brings my hands into one of his hand while his other warm hand traveling down my curves. I squirm, what is he doing?! And why am I reaction positively!?!!

His hand lifts my shirt slightly, exposing skin, and causing a snarl to erupt from me. His hand levitates on my stomach, causing heat to explode from his touch. My heart raced, my breath grows heavy, my eyes widening from horror. He bends down, whispering in my ear, "This can happen in real fights. If you get captured that is," My breath hitches, understanding what he is planning to do.

His hand runs up my shirt, and almost reaches my bra. My animal quickly takes over my body. I hiss, my eyes turning blue. I manage to elbow away his hand from going any higher. Ethan grins, removing his hand from under my shirt to hold my down my two hands separately again. I squirm more; using my shoulders and the strength my animal was giving to help me. With my blood pressure rising, I allow myself to use some hidden strength. Even if I don't get into pure bloods, I will not completely show my other side!

"What other side? I want to know!" Ethan whines in my head. I snarl back, "You'll never know!"

Snapping my leg up, I manage to kick Ethan in his thigh, causing a slight wince to appear on his perfect features. That's all I needed. Quickly pulling my body down towards my center, I manage to escape his grip. I roll over, dogging his hands, and jumping up. My eyes scan the perimeter. They land on the objects hanging from the roof.

Perfect.

"I'm not done with you yet Runner!" shouts Ethan as I feel my breath quicken. Using the extra strength in my legs I zoom past the awed faces.

"Go Kateeeee!!!!" I hear Anna shout as I look around for a path. "WHOOSH!" Ethan's face appears in front of me. "Eeek!" I screech jumping up from fright, and landing on his shoulders. His hands make a grab for me but miss me by an inch. I was already climbing onto one of the handle bars.

"You won't last long up there Runner!" He taunts, easily throwing himself on an object opposite from me. I keep moving, jumping from bar to bar to rope to object to bar again. Ethan, of course, closely following at my heels.

"Ms. Fangtooth!" I shout down, kicking off the bar and grabbing a rope. My hands burned as I slide slightly.

"What do you want Kate?" "I want the challenge to stop!" I screech, jumping onto another rope as Ethan leaped for me.

"You want to quit? Pure bloods would never do that!" "Well I'm not a pure blood! I actually have been fighting for my life for the last five years! Woah!" I duck, Ethan flying by me, "One thing I learned is if you know are going to lose the fight, you stop the fight! Either by disappearing, or in this 'nice community', eek!" I jump grabbing a pipe from the ceiling and swinging off of it, landing on a hanging piece of wood. My hands burned from all the swinging, and my breath was all but lost. I start to feel light-headed. "Since it is a nice community, I wish to stop the fight!" I pant.

I leap off the wood, front flipping to land on another hanging bar, just above the object that Ethan was on. Ms. Fangtooth grins, "Then why are you still fighting?" I shout back, grunting as I drop, punching Ethan in the stomach, and sending him flying to a bar below us. "Because you never stop fighting back until you know that you'll escape freely or win!" I snarl, flipping off the bar and landing a kick into Ethan's chest. My world goes into slow motion as Ethan is pushed away toward the ground. I feel the last of my breath leave me and I stagger against the bar. I blink a few times, my vision blurry. My lightheadedness finally gets to me. My body topples over and begins its fall toward the ground.

My eyes close and I allow myself to fall into a peaceful darkness, and to the 15-feet-away floor.

Chapter 5- Passed

"**S**PLASH!" I gasp for breath as water is dunked on top of me. My body sits straight up, though was also being held up by another source. "Omg Kate! You are okay!" Anna says, quickly lunging for a hug.

I freeze, not used to affection, before putting my hand around her giving her a hug. She grabs my shoulders and smiles, "You passed!"

"W-what?" I stammer. Anna's smile grows, "You passed the test! You made it to purebloods!"

"What!" I slowly notice the people around me. Anna was in front of me, Jack was hovering a ball of water next to me (He is probably the one who woke me), Léo was leaning against the wall. Will was gone. And Ethan, wait, where's Ethan?

A breath tickles my ear, "Over here runner..." I gasp as I hear the most annoying creature ever, Ethan. A hand moves down my back and I tense, noticing where I was sitting. Ethan was holding me up in his lap!

"W-w-what?!?" I ask mentally. "When you fell, from my poison of course, who else was there to catch you?"

"B-b-but I saw you fall!" I shriek inside my head. Ethan replies, "You saw me fall but never hit the ground."

I release a breath, annoyed, "Of course. And poison?!"

"Want to know how you passed?" grins Anna. I nod my head, shuffling uncomfortably under Ethan's hand. Though it did feel, right; almost.

"Well you pasted parts 1, 2, and 3 of the purebloods test before the second fight. Part 3 was when Ethan was using his charm and touching you to try to get you to submit. It did the opposite though. But you did surprise everyone with your climbing idea and how you lasted so long with the poison in your system. You also passed part 4 which was stopping the fight before it got out of hand, and part 5 which was not quitting until you knew the fight was over. Then you fell, passing out, and Ethan caught you."

"Ah...." I breathe out, looking at my drenched clothing. Anna squeals, "And also, we are taking you to live in our quarters!"

"What!" I shout out, jumping out of Ethan's arms. Ethan replies, "Each pack living on/near school grounds has to take a free-runner for two months. The free-runner is not allowed to not accept. If the free-runner does well, they might get into the pack. However, free-runner can choose not to join once the months are over."

I gulp, "So I am living with you guys for two months?" Jack now replies, "Yes, following our rules and commands. Ethan gets to choose who you are assigned too, and it most likely won't be a mated couple"

Well there goes my hope of being with Anna. I nod my head slowly, not liking this idea at all, but going with it, "But why did you choose me? I am a female free-runner."

Léo walks over to be in front of me as Ethan rests his back against the wall, watching me. Léo picks up Anna and gives her a kiss, then smiles at me,

"Exactly, you are a free-runner girl. You are the only free-runner female which means you have to be stronger than all the males to survive. And from your report, you are very strong."

"My report?" I ask. Jack smirks, "Ya babe, your report that tells us a little about your free-runner life. Turns out you were reported to be strong more times than everyone at this school."

"Really?" I ask my jaw dropping. I slowly start to feel the cold creep onto my wet body.

Anna shakes her head slightly, smiling, "I'm going to take her to change. She is already shivering. Come on Kate."

She takes my arm and leads me to Ms. Fangtooth, who congratulates me and teleports us to the locker rooms.

----------Ethan's p.o.v:

I watch the girls leave, my eye lingering on Kate. Such a weird girl. A slight smile reaches my lips as I remember her under me; she had such fire! Why was she turning me on so badly? I groan. It's only her first day too!

"So, who are you going to assign her to?" Léo asks. "What?" I ask, being brought back from my fantasies.

Jack snickers as I shoot him a death glare. Léo repeats, "Who are you going to assign her too? Like who is she going to live with for the next two months?"

I sigh, placing my hands behind my head and look out to the fighting arena, "I have no idea really..... Probably not one of the girls. Well, maybe Athena."

Jack snorts, "Athena is too annoying, she'll drive Kate up a wall. That's the last thing we want." I grin and catch Léo's eyes. He had the same mischievous spark in his eyes. "Oh come on, you just don't want to say you are crushing on her," I smirk.

"Hell no!" Jack instantly turns a shade of red. Léo flashes his fangs, "We all know you've got the mate bond with her, you just won't accept it."

"I'm a god! I don't have a mating bond like werewolves or animal transformers!" Jack shouts, annoyed.

Léo snickers as I grin, "We all have mating bonds. It's just harder for vampires, demigods, and fairies to feel them."

"By the way, am I'm sensing a slight bond with you and Kate?" smirks Jack, leaning against the wall, and successfully changing the subject.

"What!" I scream in my head but reply smoothly, "I don't think so....." Jack laughs, "Ya, because we all know you have a bond with Sheila." I growl, glaring at Jack.

Léo mumbles under his breath, "Speaking of the devil," as a high pitched voice shrieks, "Ethan! Baby-boo!" I curse under my breath as the figure of Sheila runs up to us.

"What do you want Sheila?" I ask, annoyed. "Baby-boo, I want your love, as always!" She whines.

I catch Jack's and Léo's eyes, and nod slightly.

"I'd love to stay and chat, Sheila, but I have to change." I quickly stand up, passing her without another glance.

My friends follow me, quickly getting teleported into the locker room. I sigh, leaning against a locker behind me.

"There is no way in hell I'm doing that!" I grin as I hear Kate's thoughts in my head. I sigh, this will only last 24 hours, but it's still as fun as hell to mess with.

"Why not?" I reply mentally to her. "GET OUT OF MY HEAD ETHAN!" I hear her scream from the other side of the wall.

I chuckle as I hear Anna asking what's wrong. I send a quick message to Anna at what's happening and hear her laugh. Now, where am I going to place wild Kate? Hmm........

Hey everyone :P.

Its New Years tomorrow and that is what I celebrate, so...... MULTIPLE CHAPTER UPDATE

Sorry Again, and ENJOY!

(Last Edited Chapter)

Chapter 6- Home

Kate p.o.v

The rest of my classes were a blur. They were all really boring and no fun. It was just rules, rules, rule, another rule, and more rules. God it sucks. But it is even scarier now that they are over, I somehow have to sneak away. I am not staying at that pack house! I wait for the bus, hidden in the forest, just listening to the world around me.

I lean against a tree, listening to make sure no one was following me. My legs were crossed, and my shoulder held all my weight. The bus zooms in, and squeals to a stop.I sigh, almost there. My feet crunch the leaves underneath me as I walk steadily toward the bus.

"Where you goin' runner?" Ethan's voice comes from behind me."Shit!" I mentally cuss, freezing in my tracks. My heart races as he comes up behind me.

"Now now runner, what did I tell you about cussing?" Ethan says in my head, coming closer to me until I feel his breath tickling my ear. I gulp, tensing, "I'm going on the bus." Then snarling, "Get out of my head!"

He chuckles, one of his hands playing with a strand of my frizzy hair. "It's time to go home, little one." His breath gave me ice cold shivers as he leaned closer to my skin, kissing his bite. I feel my breath get heavy, how is he doing this to my body! I have been with tons of other guys who had tried to do this with me, all of them quickly learned never to do it again. Usually because they ended up in the hospital or dead.

"Remember Runner, I am a vampire, that is one of my tricks. Both tracking you by using my bite and making you feel this way........"he whispers in my head. I feel my heart race, tracking me?!?

"Come on, let's go home....." He whispers, pulling away and giving a slight tug to my hair. I sigh, defeated. Turning on my heal, I follow him through the woods, noticing how he makes no sound compared to my stomping. My eyes scan the forest as we go. Large pines, maple trees, and leaves covering the floor in a blanket.

He all of a sudden breaks to a stop, my body crashing into his. My feet loose their balance on the slippery leaves and I feel myself tip backward. "Woah!" I yell, falling backward. My body tenses as something catches it. I peep open an eye to find Ethan holding me by my waist, amused. Such a clíche moment.

I suck in a breath as I remove myself from that position. Too awkward, too romantic.Ethan sniggers, "Don't like romance do we, runner?" He sends me an air kiss before smirking and turning away to continue the walk toward my new home.

Cocky vampire!I growl, my eyes scanning the floor for something to chuck at him.Perfect! My hand grabs the rough pine cone, weighing it. I grin watching Ethan's bobbing head. I fling the pine cone to Ethan's Raven hair with deadly accuracy.

With an easy dodge, he flips around smirking, "Missed me. You got to try harder runner."I grin back, watching the pine cone bounce from tree to tree, "Don't need too...."

"SMACK!" The pine cone collided with Ethan's head making a satisfying crack. Ethan grabs the back of his head in pain, his eyes squeezed shut. He takes a deep inhale before snapping open his eyes, "What the f*ck?" He asks, angry. He takes a step toward me, his eyes red.

He was scary looking, but I was quickly taken in with the victory of revenge. I tilt my head, a smile from ear to ear, "Don't cuss, vampire...." I snap back, crossing my arms in victory.

---------------Ethan P.O.V

Oh f*ck no, did she just use that line on me? I chuckled inwardly at her snappiness, but defiantly not liking it. I grit my teeth, trying to control my anger. The pounding where the pine cone hit me was not helping either. I scan her petite body. Her wild hair to one side as she looks so proud for that move. She looks so confident behind those crossed arms, and smug smile. I have to admit it was a good move. I did not expect for the pine cone to bounce off trees. I sigh, noticing her uncomfortableness with me staring at her, with only a glare on my face.

A laughs breaks us both from our emotions, "You finally found someone to challenge you back, ey Ethan?" I feel my features soften, smirking at the voice, "What makes you so confident that she is challenging me?"

Athena laughs, flipping off one pine tree branch to the next. Her wild golden brown hair billowing as her green-blue eyes scanned the scene below, "she seems too confident and you not so sure, pack-daddy."

I groan, "Not you too!" She smirks, doing a final flip to land on the ground, "yes Anna told me of your little 'nickname'." She looks toward Kate, watching her carefully.

Kate shuffles a bit, uncomfortable. I smirk, that's the last thing Athena is, uncomfortable. Athena sticks out her hand, as I lean against the tree. It's not like I have anything better to do."My name's Athena, Anna told me a little about you," she says. Kate looks discouraged but eventually takes Athena's hand cautiously and shakes it. I have to admit, Athena did look dangerous today. She had two hunting knifes on her belt, her face was stained with dirt and mud. Her clothing was all tight camo outfits, with black lines under her eyes like football players. Her hair was messy and her green eyes wild.

"I'm Kate...." Kate mumbles, unsure. I sigh,"Time to save her," I think to myself, pushing myself off the tree. "Going hunting Athena?" I ask, my eyes turning to their normal blue shade. She grins, turning toward me, "Yep! But I had to ask you first...So that..."I interrupt her, smirking, "So your parents blame me and not you."She shines me a mischievous grin, "you betcha!"

I roll my eyes, amused, "Alright go, but be home before 4 o'clock, alright?"She nods and was quickly gone, running through the peaceful forest. I watch her leave until I feel a slight heat source next to me. I look down at Kate, she was now almost pressed against me.

I smirk, "Scared are we runner?" Her fire instantly lights up, "I'm not scared! I just don't like strangers," she mumbles. God I love how she does that.

"Come on then, let's make the rest of the pack not strangers," I laugh, beginning to walk the familiar path to my house. Soon the trail comes to view and I leave Kate to her own thoughts. It's soooo hard not to eavesdrop on her thoughts, especially since her fire is also in her thoughts.

"Kate we are here," I say, bringing her out of her head. I don't exactly want her to crash into me, though secretly, I kinda do. I feel the familiar buzz of my pack mates. Will's, Athena's, and Sheila, buzzes were distant. Léo's and

Anna's buzz was more intensified. They were probably upstairs. Linda was also upstairs. I feel for Jack's buzz. It instantly comes pounding in me. I sigh and send a telepathic message to Jack, "Stop messing with the buzzes Jack!" I shake my head, annoyed. He actually knows how to change his buzz to mess with me. Moving aside branch, I allow Kate to see the house.I smirk as her jaw drops, "Welcome to our home!"

Kate's p.o.v

My jaw drops as my eyes catch the house's full glory. Pardon me, the mansion's full glory. It was huge, very styled and modern. It also had this homie cabin look. I glance sideways at Ethan's. He was smirking at my reaction. I quickly shut my mouth, getting rid of emotions from my features. His smirk only grows.

"Come on, I'll take you around," he leads me to the house. I quietly follow, not liking this feeling of being a dog.

He unlocks the house, opening the door to allow me to come in. My eyes grow huge in wonder. The inside was even cooler that the outside! It still had that cabin look, but it had more 21st century stuff. My eyes travel the down stairs. To my left, a dining room, to my front a huge kitchen (happy dance here), and to my left, the living room with Jack on the plush black sofa, watching tv. My mouth drops at the size of everything here; it's huge.

I hear keys being thrown onto a counter and I turn back toward the kitchen.Ethan asks smugly, "like it, runner?" I nod, still in wonder. Ethan smirks, watching me as I scan the area. I take a seat infront of the granite counter in one of those spinning red stools.

I watch Ethan putting away things for a little before hearing Jack sigh.I swivel in my chair, happily, swinging my legs until I catch Jack's eyes, "What's wrong?" I ask.

Jack smirks, finally seeing me, "Welcome home, runner. And nothing, there isn't anything on tv that's all...." He sighs, annoyed.

Ethan playfully snaps back, "Then you should go do your homework!"Jack whines, "but I want to go give her the tour!"Ethan rolls his eyes, "Go!"Jack winks at me, "I can give you a private tour of my room later. We can inspect the bedroom door and have your cloths decorate the floor.

My mouth drops, and my cheeks warm up. I then smirk, "Totally, I'm sure Athena would love that. Should I invite her too?" Jack hesitates as Ethan bursts out laughing, "The runner got you Jack...."

Jack mumbles something under his breath. Ethan starts to laugh harder, catching what he said. "Okay I'm going to my room," Jack grumbles, standing up and walking toward the stairs.

I watch him go before spinning in my chair again, laughing. Ethan watches me amused, leaning against the counter. "Come on runner, might as well get you familiar with the house."

Chapter 7- Old Friends, New Friends

The house, I mean mansion, is absolutely huge! The downstairs has three guest rooms, plus all the necessary rooms like a kitchen and dining room. Sheila lives in one of the guest bedrooms. Thank goodness, because otherwise I would kill her in her sleep.

However, now, I am following Ethan up the modern glass steps to the second floor. The upstairs still has that cabin look. I feel my blood pressure rise from excitement. Hey don't judge, I haven't lived in a house in a while. As we walk through, I see a bunch of doors, which are, apparently, closets.

We crash into Léo and Anna as we travel the rooms, but still continue the tour. The first room on the left was actually Léo's/Anna's room. It was jungle themed; Trees, vines, and lush pillows decorated the place. Then came Linda's and Will's room.

I peak my head into the room, my body hanging sideways from the door-frame. Ethan smirks as he steps into the room, "Hey Linda."

Linda, the small female on the bed, jolts. The room itself was this mix of forest and pink look. Surprisingly, it looked good. It also had a huge window that showed the nobel mountains and forest.

"Oh! Ethan! I did not hear you....." She says quietly with a smile. Her eyes land on me and horror fixes her face.She randomly 'eeps', I guess, then yellow power flushes around her, causing her to disappear.

"Ha-choo!" I sneeze as the dust tickles my nose. Ethan laughs, "Linda, relax, this is our free-runner, Kate."

She randomly appears behind me causing a shriek from me. She jumps back in fear. Her cheeks flush, "Sorry, I'm just a little shy, but I'm Linda, a fairy."

"Uh, Kate....." I say, looking over this girl. She had a small frame with blonde curls and shy blue eyes. "Nice to meet you, Kate." She says with a small smile. Then, to Ethan, she says, "I need to go finish my fairy studies; tell me when Will comes home."

Ethan nods, letting her go into her room before shutting the door and grinning at me. "What?" I ask, confused. He shakes his head, still smiling, "Nothing, come on."

I keep following him. Jack's and Athena's room are conjoined, but separated by a wall. Both had this rich God look, though Athena's had a more tomboy look to it. Ethan's room I loved the most. My mouth fell into a smile as I stepped into the drafty room.

To my left a huge balcony taking up the whole wall and to my right a desk with a dark lush bed. However, his room kept the cabin look, but had a more powerful vibe.

He sniggers, "I see you like this room...""What? How does he know!" I scream inside my head.He laughs, "Again, forgot something?"

I facepalm myself and he bursts out laughing, "Nice, runner." I feel my skin heat in anger. I hate when people make fun of me. "I'm not making fun of you, I'm just messing with you." He sneers. "Okay see that door there--" he points to a dark wood door. I nod my head.

"That's your room. My room is a conjoined room, so you get the conjoined part." I freeze, "I'm living with YOU?" My mouth drop. He smirks, "What don't like me, runner?"

I mumble, turning away, "Not really...." He grins. I gasp as he comes face-to-face to me. His powerful blue eyes holding my simple brown ones. My heart races from the shock, and my breath gets heavy. Stupid super speed!

I feel one of Ethan's hand go around my waist and his other pet my cheek as his head leans in so his mouth was next to my ear. "Oh runner, what fun we can have here....." He whispers. I gulp, feeling an uneasy sensation in my stomach. I hear him lick his lips as my brain tries to function.

I push my hands against his chest. Holy freak! Those abs! I push against him, "Ethan s-stop...." I have trouble whispering out.

"It seems like your body doesn't want me to stop, runner." His hand travels up and down my curves causing shivers from me. His icy breath tickling my ear, causing my brain too loose its ability to work.

"E-E-Ethan...." I say, out of breath. I push against him harder, but with no avail. He was a prison, holding me against him. My animal side started to prowl, not like this.

I allow some strength to go into my arms. "Ethan!" I say. This time, with more worry as he begins to travel kisses down my neck. I start to squirm, noticing my body reacting positively to this movement. So my voice catches a more fearful tone, "Ethan!"

I pull my body down, causing me to slip free. Quickly crawling away, away from those arms, I hear Ethan laugh. "Why are you so fun to tease, runner?" He asks, amused."What?" I ask, confused, still blushing deeply. He laughs again, "You are fun to tease."

I instantly turn red figuring out that this is a joke. My mood becomes dark, "That was cruel."He smirks, "That's what you get for 'not really' liking me."I take a deep inhale, glaring at him.

He smiles, "The rest of the group is here, let's go meet them."I hesitate, but eventually storm out, following Ethan out the doorway and to the downstairs.

What's happening to me?

--------Ethan's p.o.v.Well, maybe it wasn't a joke, but it started as one. I used one of my vampire powers to cause her to go into a more fragile state, and a more lustful state. But somehow, she used it against me. I went into lust mode. It was like it bounced off of her and went into me. I inwardly groan, remembering how this girl turned me on.

I sigh, feeling all the buzzes of my pack. All of them were downstairs and Kate was silent walking behind me. She was probably planning revenge. I laugh, of course she is!

I lead her downstairs and to the living room."Baby-Boo!" A high pitched voice shrills. My features instantly go into a frown, not this again. This girl won't f*cking leave me alone!

I respond, mono-tone, "Hi Sheila....." "Hey baby," her boring eyes travel past me and to Kate. She instantly frowns. "Who's this?" She snarls.

I open my mouth but am quickly interrupted by Kate, "I'm the new runner, Sheila!" Kate hisses. Woah! Where did that fire and hate come from?

I nod my head, not wanting any fights today, "Now Sheila, if you don't mind. I must introduce our runner to the rest of the pack."

I push past her getting grins of approval from Léo and Jack. They hate Sheila also. I grin back as I walk down onto the carpeted floor, in front of the tv, facing the dark long couch(well it was more 3 long couches put together in a half circle almost). Kate follows me, though with more unease.

I chuckle slightly as I gesture to her, "Everyone, this is Kate, she is our free-runner for these two months." "Hey Kate!" Everyone responds with enthusiasm, except Sheila. Jealous werewolf.

She bows her head slightly, doing the nervous shuffle, "hi."I smirk, looking at her. God she is so wild and strong, yet so fragile; almost. My head turns back to the pack that is lounging around on the huge couches, "as we all know, tonight's movie night. So, who is the last person on our list?"

Jack snickers, "It's you, dumb*ss." I see Kate hold back a giggle.

She has cute giggle. Are you serious Ethan, that has to be the first thing that comes to mind! Ugh.

"Alright, so Kate, every Monday and Friday we have this thing called movie night. That's when a person picks a movie and we all watch it."

Athena pipes up, "We also have game night!"I give her a look and continue, "Yes, we also have game nights every Wednesday and Saturday... But anyway, your turn to pick a movie will be after I do..."Kate nods her head, "okay, I'm cool with that."

Sheila snarls, "Why does she get to choose? It's not like she is in the pack!"I growl, getting protective over Kate. Wait, why am I getting protective? It's only her 1st day!

Anna snarls back, allowing her leopard teeth to show, "She is part of this pack until the two months are over and she chooses not to be apart of it!" Yes! Thats my girl! Well, best friend's girl. I silently cheer.

"Alright, so whose turn is it today?" I ask, getting back on topic. Jack shoots his hand up, "my turn! I choose Pitch Perfect!"

The group laughs and gets settled in as Linda uses her magic to put Pitch Perfect onto the screen. The movie plays, and I get absorbed into it. Ignoring the jealous looks Sheila was sending me, and enjoying Kate's presence next to me.

Hey guys! I know this is kinda slow chapter, but I promise it'lll get better! This chapter was needed to introduce the ways of the pack house.

Please comment suggestions and opinions on the book. Thanks for the reads guys, it means a lot! <3

Enjoy

Chapter 8- Movie Night

Ethan's p.o.v

Kate really seems to enjoy movie nights. It's her second week here and she was quickly accustomed. Athena, Anna, Linda and her have quickly become best friends,Which I am happy for.

It's Friday and we are all settled into the living room. I glance around the room as Linda starts to work her magic, putting "Men in Black," onto the dark screen; Athena's choice.

A sleek gorgeous leopard lay comfortably on the floor with a huge black maned lion curled protectively around her. Both Léo and Anna were purring. This was their favorite position during movie night.

Athena was on the middle couch, one leg hanging off the couch while the other bent close to her. Jack was sitting outstretched on the other side, trying to hide his glances to Athena. Will and Linda were cuddling together on the right hand couch, enjoying each other. Kate was joining me on my couch, the left hand side couch. We were sitting on opposite ends. I smirk at how uncomfortable she looked.

Sheila had stormed to her room, leaving us in peace. I hear Kate sigh, "is this how you guys live all the time?"

I smile slightly, my voice going to a whisper, "Kind of.... It gets more fun during real weekends."She furrows her eyebrows, her eyes still on the tv, "Real weekends?"I nod, "when we go out to the forest to play....""Shhhh!" Jack snarls as the movie plays.

Kate makes an 'o' shape in understanding. Her attention quickly gets absorbed by the movie and she relaxes. I allow my eyes to linger on her. I watch as her face change; she had her cheering face, her sad face, her happy face, her confused face, her adventurous face, and ect. It was interesting.

I watch the movie in peace, though many times have no idea what's happening; usually my head was whirling about Kate. Ugh, her scent is soooo addicting. I am an alpha, I do have that familiar reminder to get an alpha female; and imprint on her. It's kind of disguising, but first I need to find my mate, which is hard, for I am a vampire. But I'm wondering if Kate might be it.

However, I do enjoy Kate's little shows on her face. I can't read her head anymore, which I want to do sooo badly. It is so fun teasing her with her own thoughts. But for now, I just get to guess.

At one point of the movie she grabs my arm in fear. I inwardly laugh. So strong yet scared of movies.I smirk, clearing my throat. She looks toward me and instantly blushes when she sees that she was grabbing me. Her small soft hand quickly leaves mine as she keeps turning redder and redder. She brushes her hair forward to hide her scarlet face. Too late sugar.I chuckle, going back to the movie. Though, I do miss the contact.

Before long, half the movie was gone. The two large felines were peacefully snoozing, circled next to each other. Linda fell asleep on Will's shoulder and Will looks like he is about to pass out.

Jack had this happy glow on his face. Athena was asleep on his lap, peacefully. He kept gently petting her. A smile was clearly imprinted on his face.

I smirk, catching his attention, then pointing to Athena. He rolls his eyes, trying to hide his embarrassment. He then mischievously smiles and points to my lap.

I instantly tense. Kate was asleep on me! How did I not notice this?!Hesitantly, I remove my hand from her back. What do I do with this girl? I'm usually smooth with girls. However, with this one, I don't even know what to do with her sleeping on me!

Jack chuckles, allowing his attention to go back to the TV. I carefully put my hand back on Kate. She slightly pushes towards it. Hmm that's weird. I sigh, noticing how all the girls were asleep. Must have been a hard day in magic. (Yes, it's an all girls class... Just don't ask me how I know)

I sigh, before clearing my throat. Will stirs and looks up at me, his eyes pretty much closed. I trace out with my lips, "Bed time!"He nods groggily, shaking Linda slightly to wake her. She yawns, flicking her hand to turn off the tv and snapping her fingers to teleport her and Will to their room.

I catch Jack's eyes, then look down to the cats. He sighs, before finally taking a pillow and tossing it to the horse sized lion. Léo jolts up, his hair sticking up like a cat. A low growl emits through his throat in surprise. He looks from me and Jack to me again. "Bed time," I whisper, knowing he would hear me. The lion, or Léo, nods his head, gently nudging Anna awake. Anna yawns, showing her many sharp teeth before rising up to her paws and trotting away with Léo behind her.

I give a nod to Jack and he sighs. His arm snakes to under Athena's knees, and under her back. He heaves her up, grunting at her weight, but eventually carries her limp body away, bridal style.

I sigh, listening to the peaceful breathing of Kate, watching her chest move up and down. Finally, I tear myself away from the show and pick her up with ease; also bridal style.

Super-speeding to my room, to make no noise, I quickly place Kate down on my bed. Wait. No. She goes in the other room.

Eh whatever.I bite my lip. Unsure whether to undress her or not. No, she'll kill me if I do.I smile slightly in pleasure, watching her sleeping state. I know, stalkerish, but still.

I tuck her away, gently placing her head on a pillow.

When she finally was settled in my bed, I collapse on the comfy mattress. I sigh, looking up to the dark ceiling. It's almost the weekend. Will Kate be able to keep up during our 'real weekend'? My eyes travel to her sleeping form. She was so tense. She nudges closer to me, wanting my warmth. I feel a slight smile tug my lip.

I look back at the empty ceiling. This girl is changing me.....

My mind fills up with questions and thoughts as slowly darkness takes over me and I leave to go into dream world.

Chapter 9- Cooking Relationships

Kate's p.o.v

I stretch out across the silky bed, my eyes still not opening from the great night I had. God, magic class did wear me out.

Hold up. I'm in a bed?!?

I shriek slightly as I roll off the unfamiliar bed. Gasping as the air gets knocked out of my lungs as my back meets the floor. I freeze, the darkness of the room enveloping me.

"Kate?" Asks an amused voice.

I don't respond, freezing in fear.

"Kate I know it's you. You are the only one that even enters this room. That, and your heartbeat is really loud." The amused voice continues.

I gulp, no it's not! Stupid heart! Stop beating so fast!

The voice sighs before I hear a body shuffle on the bed that I was just in. Wait, where am I anyway?

"Ah!" I screech as Ethan's head pops up from the bed. "Thud!" My head smashes against the table next to the bed. Fuuu.....

I hiss in pain as I grasp the backside on my head; it sizzling with pain.

My memory comes back: I'm at the pack house. I look down at my body, still clothed. Thank god, otherwise I would have shredded someone.

Ethan smirks, "Bravo runner,"

I roll my eyes, standing up, "Not my fault I thought you were some rapist or drunk dude that brought me into his bed."

Ethan smirk deepens, "How are you sure? Maybe I am a drunk dude that brought you into his bed....."

I scoff, "Ya, sure..."

Ethan opens his mouth to make a remark but I interrupt him, "Imma go change," I say, waving my hand behind me as I storm my way to the dark wood door that lead to my room. My head still stung.

Slamming the door, I lean against it. What even happened last night?

I shake my head, I don't want to even know. Going through my closet, I realize I don't have anything to wear. Well, it's not like I could afford to carry or even buy anything else.

I sigh, grabbing my only other shirt and pair of jeans and throwing them on the bed. Slipping out of my current clothes, I quickly change into my other pair.

I throw my hair into a messy pony-tail before storming out of my room.

My jaw drops.

In front of my stood Ethan, shirtless. I feel my cheeks heat as he catches my eyes, slipping on his shirt. He had toned muscles and a nice 6 pack with everything else included.

"Enjoying the view?" He smirks, finishing pulling down his shirt over his head.

I turn away, blushing deeply. I then feel my animal side give me courage. I raise my head up to meet Ethan's eyes and smirk, "Well of course..."

He hesitates, confusion holding his face, "W-what?"

I smirk before walking up to him, swaying my hips slightly. He freezes, gulping, as I stop in front of him.

I lean up, as if I am about to go for a kiss before whispering, "I got you, blood-sucker...."

I gentle allow my hand to travel down his chest, smirking at his shaky reaction, "I got you, and I will always get my revenge...."

I lean in closer, kissing his cheek, before rapidly pulling away, leaving poor Ethan completely stuck in confusion and regret. He looks at me with pleading eyes to continue but I smirk, giving him a hint.

He frowns, "This was a trick wasn't it..."

I give a slight smile, mischiefs shinning in my eyes, "Revenge, blood-sucker, sweet cold-hearted revenge..."

I see him tense from slight anger/annoy. I blow a kiss to him before quickly running out of the room, slamming the door shut behind me and bursting into a full sprint downstairs. I giggle all the way down to the kitchen grabbing Anna's shoulders and hiding behind them.

"Kate!" Ethan's voice rings out around the house.

I bite my lip with a smile, still hidden behind Anna.

She smirks, "What did you do?"

"Revenge," I chuckle, holding onto her shoulders tightly. She laughs, allowing me to use her as my shield.

"Kate...." A sing-songy voice rings out, coming from a person going down the stairs; Ethan, of course.I giggle, this is so fun!! I love revenge!

"Ethan? Baby? What's the matter?" A annoying voice asks, stopping Ethan.

I smirk at the groan Ethan was holding back as Sheila came to view.

"Go away Sheila!" He growls.

She crosses her arms, "No! I demand to know what is going on! I am your mate, baby! Shouldn't I get your love and attention?"

I roll my eyes, leaving my shield, Anna, knowing Ethan won't be able to come any further downstairs.

"You are not my mate!" He shouts, storming back upstairs.

I couldn't help but grin. I lean against the counter, watching as Sheila enters the kitchen.

I glare at her, remembering clearly her face when I was sent off. She stops in front of me, glaring at me with arms crossed. Anna stood tense by my side, though she was getting supplies out.

"Ethan is mine! Understand that b*tch?" She says annoyed.

I snarl back, "Everything is always yours, you spoiled little brat. Time to learn how what it feels like to have competition, Princess!

Her mouth drops a little in anger. Apparently the pack was too nice to tell her the straight on truth. She composes herself before raising her head higher and storming away from the kitchen, shouting, "I will tell my mommy and dad!!!"

I scoff, rolling my eyes as Anna claps slowly. "Nobody has ever called her a brat before..." She chuckles.

I shrug, "Hey, she is..." I lean over, quickly grabbing the egg from Anna's hand.

She purses her lips in anger and confusion. I give a slight smile, "Relax, I'm cooking breakfast today. You deserve it. That and I haven't cooked in a while."

Her mood instantly lights up, "Alright! Sounds good!"

She takes a seat at one of the swiveling stools, leaning against the granite counter.

My hands start to work like magic as all my memories on cooking come back to me. Before I knew it, I was happily running around the kitchen cooking multiple meals and breakfasts at once.

Anna kept me entertained and reminded me of things here and there. I on the other hand gave her tips and tricks. Linda soon joined, quietly watching with a small smile. Then Athena, who joined into our conversation smoothly.

I listened to the girls as the three pans in front of me, sizzled.

"Oh my freaking Magic, what is that smell?" A new voice says.

I turn around, holding one of the pans in my hand while a spatula in the other.

"That's you cooking?" Jack says, his mouth falling open.

I roll my eyes, turning back to the stove. I smugly reply as I hear him grunt from Athena's kick, "Yes. Just because I am a free-runner doesn't mean I can't cook. Doesn't ever female need to know to cook?"

"Well, every wife does....." He begins. I smirk as he gets a harder kick from Athena. I wink at him as he clutches his place in pain, no sound coming out of his mouth. He purses his lips and manages to whisper out, "you did that on purpose..."

I laugh slightly as I watch Léo come down the stairs, filling his nose with the scent of my cooking, "Maybe I did Jack, maybe I did."

Léo quickly lifts Anna up from her stool, causing giggles from her, and puts her in his lap, "This looks so delicious Kate..." He says, eyeing the food hungrily. He reaches forward to pluck a tomato from one of the plates.

I slap his hand away, "No harassing the food mister!" I grab the plates, putting them on another counter.

Léo playfully whines, "Aw, come on!"

I glare at Anna. "Get your boyfriend under control!" I laugh.

She chuckles slightly, leaning her head back to give him a kiss. Jack grunts as he gets up on one of the stools next to Athena.

As we hear two people running down the stairs, Athena smiles, "I can't wait to try it Kate!"

"Damn it!" Ethan groans, seeing me with a frying pan on one hand, a spatula in the other, and a little apron on me. Will tilts his head slightly to me before walking toward Linda and placing her in his lap. She giggles before giving him a kiss. Ethan continues grumbling"Now I can't get my revenge on you for everyone wants to eat!"

I smirk, flipping the eggs, causing an applause to go through the crowd. "Oh no, looks like I have to please you with food. Don't I, blood-sucker."

Athena and Jack go into snickers.

Ethan sighs, playing along and taking another seat at the granite table, "It looks like you win, servant..."

"Ooo! You did not just use that card, playboy!" I say, my mouth falling open.

The crowd goes into laughs, "Nice Ethan, now you are going to make her kill you in your sleep!" laughs Jack. Athena and Anna nod in agreement while Léo, Will, and Linda just grin.

Ethan shrugs, "Eh, I can get away with it, right servant?"

"If this food wasn't for the other people in the pack including you, I would have dumped it on your head and stuck the hot frying pan down your shirt..."I reply smoothly, continuing to finish up my many plates of food. I am just in a too good of a mood to have that affect me.

Ethan smirks.

"Mmm! That smells and looks sooooo good Kate!" Anna says, her mouth watering as I place down her plate.

I pretty much created a normal breakfast. Eggs, sausages, toast, but also added other small things too. Like little recipes I know up my sleeve. I also gave each person a twist. For example, Anna's and Léo's eggs have different meats on them, though Léo's also has hot sauce. Linda and Will had certain jams. However, to Linda's, I added some lavender flowers to the side it make it more 'her'. Jack and Athena the same. I finish setting up the last plate, pouring into a cup some blood from the fridge, before putting it down in front of Ethan.

I gasp as I feel his hand brush over mine. I catch his electrifying eyes, noticing the slight mischief spark at my reaction. He genuinely smiles, "Thank you for breakfast, Kate..."

Did he just call me Kate, and not runner?

I pull my hand away, stammering slightly, before catching myself. I smile back, "Your welcome, blood-sucker..."

He grins, digging into his food. I sigh, leaning over the counter, watching as the pack gobbled up their food hungrily and happily.

"Oh god, Kate, this is amazing!" Moans Anna through bites of food. I smile, "Thanks...."

Linda asks, "Aren't you going to eat anything?"

I shake my head no, "I don't do anything in this house or earn money. I can't pay for the food so...."

Will interrupts, mad, "Bullsh*t! You are part of this pack, and you get to eat with it! Plus, you have done a lot, like give us breakfast and challenge Ethan!"

The group goes into laughs as I smile at Will, "Thanks."

He nods his head before the temptation of the food gets to him and he goes back to digging in.

I make myself some quick normal eggs, and eat standing as we all finish breakfast. Today is starting off like a good day.

Chapter 10- Brother

I sigh, dropping off my backpack onto the floor and collapsing onto the couch. Today's school was okay. Though Magic class sucked as always. I glance up at the clock watching the seconds tick away.

3, 2, 1, and go!

Jack flings the door open, right on my count. He walks in, making it over-exaggerating, as he leads the rest of the boys in with smug smile on his face. Linda, Anna, and Athena had to stay after for the Magic Project (Which I finished last week).

I give a slight smirk as the boys collapse onto the couches around me, "Fun day at Power class?"

Léo groans as Jack rolls his eyes. Ethan walks into the doorway a few seconds later. I watch him as he makes his way over to my couch collapsing onto the middle where my legs lay.

"Hey!" I shout, pulling my legs away. "I was sitting here!"

He smirks, "It's my house runner, I can choose where I sit..."

"Hmph! It doesn't me you have to sit on me!" I huff.

He goes into a mischievous grin. My eyes widen in fear, "No no no! Don't you dare actually sit on me!"

His grin depends as he stands up. I yelp, jumping onto the floor.

He smirks, sitting back down to the couch and stretching out onto it, taking all the room.

I growl, falling onto the carpeted floor to rest. He says smugly, "You can sit on my lap if you want."

"Like I said: I. Don't. LIKE. You." I snarl playfully, before standing up and walking over to the kitchen. Annoying freaking cocky vampire Prince! I begin to cook something up for dinner, allowing my thoughts to wonder.

------Sometime later----

Athena's laugh echoes the kitchen as the rest of the gang piles in, allowing me to be in the conversation.

"O.m.g. I just realized something! I haven't called my sister since school started!" Will pipes up.

Hmm, my own brother hasn't called me since the school year too. I wonder how he is doing. I haven't seen him for five years, ever since the night I was sent away, but I still have his number.

I smile, putting my cake to bake in the oven as I turn up the heat slightly on my spaghetti and tomato sauce.

Will pulls out his phone as the gang take their seats at the granite table. Anna and Léo together as always and Linda in Will's lap. Ethan was watching the pack with a smile next to Jack. Jack was next to Athena, casting glances at her.

Will pulls out his iPhone, beginning to search for his sister's number. The group waits patiently, laughing here and there.

He puts the phone to his ear as it starts ringing.

"RING RING RING! RING RING RING!" My phone goes off. I laugh, "Wow, such a coincidence!"

The group chuckles, going back to waiting for Will's sister to pick up as I place down my mixing spoon and go for my backpack.

Unzipping my backpack, I grab my phone and see my brother's number pop up.

I turn to the waiting gang, "I got to take this." They wave me off with ease as I go into one of the guest bedrooms and pick up the phone.

"Hey bro!" I happily say.

"Hey sis, how's it hanging?"

I sigh, "Eh, alright. I was taken into this pack at my new school..."

"That's great! Now you don't have to be a free-runner anymore!"

I scoff slightly, "I'm not sure I want to join. Plus, I have to wait two months anyway..."

William, my brother laughs on the other line, "Sounds a lot like a free-runner we got in our pack."

I smile slightly, "so... any news?"

"Actually ya! I forgot to tell you, I got a mate!"

I smile, "Really!? That's awesome! Is she a werewolf?"

William chuckles, "No, actually a fairy. Say hi, honey..."

A distance, quiet voice starts to bicker slightly. She sounded nice enough. I heard Athena laugh from outside my door. However, then I hear someone laugh exactly like her from my phone.

I feel my heart speed increase, "Uh, William, you do go by the nickname of Will right? And go to Mythical Academy, right?"

William chuckles slightly on the other line, "Ya, why?"

"Just making sure, and, um, last question."

"Ya?"

"Do you have a vampire as pack alpha?"

Dead silence is heard. Even the people in the background were quiet. I strain my ears, noticing no sound is coming from my 'pack'.

William's tone gets deadly, "Yes, why? And how do you know?"

I gulp slightly, "Um, William, do you have a living room?"

I hear him relax slightly, "Ya, why?"

"Can you please go there for a second?"

He chuckles slightly, before talking to his group, "I got to go to the living room, I'll be right back..."

I hear him stand up from his stool and begin walking. I sigh, feeling my breath quicken.

I quietly open the door to the guest room and make my way to the living room.

Will smiles, "Hey Kate, I'm here to my sister's request." He smiles.

"Hey Kate, I'm here to my sister's request," my phone says from William's line.

I instantly pale, "W-William?" My voice breaks.

"Kathy?" Will's mouth drops, "Y-you are K-Kate?"

"And y-you are my little brother, W-William?"

We freeze, holding each other's eyes in surprise, regret, happiness, confusion, and sadness. "Hey guys what's happening?" asks Jack as the rest of the group piles in.

"Hey guys, what's happening?" My phone echoes. The phone slips my hand from shock. It bounces on the floor, it being clearly heard from the silence in the room.

Instantly, the mood becomes darker. All eyes go to me, though I was still staring at Will, feeling my eyes getting watery.

"W-will?" My voice breaks, and I burst into tears.

"Kathy, or Uh, Kate!" He rushes over to me, enveloping me into hug. I cry into his shoulder, "oh, I've missed you so much!"

He smiles slightly, petting my back, "I promised to take care of myself, and I did, just for you."

I let out another sob. I stay like that, taking in my brother's presents for a few moments. I take a deep breath and pull away as Linda comes over, looking confused.

"W-what's going on honey?"

Will turns to face his mate, smiling, "Linda, remember that sister I told you about?"

She nods her head, blinking as things started to click.

William chuckles slightly, pointing to me, "That's her..."

~~~~~~

Next update: 1/22/14
~~~~~~

Chapter 11- Scars

M y pack became fish. All staring at me wide-eyed and open mouthed. Sheila broke the tension.

"I knew I recognized you from somewhere!"

I flip around, a snarl pasted on my face, "Ya, long time no see! Sister!"

She frowns, walking around me, "Last time I saw you, we were sending you to Mythical School. Then the system broke down and that was the last we heard from you. But now you are back," she snarls, "And I was so happy you were gone too! Did you escape cowardly when the school broke down?"

"Wait, didn't the Mythical School break down several years ago?" asks Ethan, getting slightly in the edge, sensing a fight.I grin wickedly, feeling my blood pressure rise from Sheila's words, "Who do you think caused the break-down of the school?"She bears her teeth as I glare daggers at her.

The group takes a slight step back at my words. Everyone knew about the amazing unbroken school; until of course, I broke it. Though nobody knew for I blended in with other escapees.Will starts up, awakening and whinnying slightly, "Why did you leave sister? Why didn't you come back to Dan?"

The mention of my father's name sparked a new flame inside me, "Don't you ever speak of his name!" I hiss, enraged, "He is not my father!!!"

The pack winces at my tone but continues on watching the fight between me and Sheila, hungry for my history.

Sheila crosses her arms, "So, sister, enjoyed your stay?" I snap back, "Yes, in fact, I loved it so much I ran out!"Sheila scoffs, "I don't believe you. Nobody could break their system."

I allow my eyes to show a spark of revenge and sadistic pleasure, "You'll be surprised..."I allow my eyes to flash blue then back brown, getting the same shocked reaction from Sheila as the day I left her. She quickly gathers herself back up. Her eyes tinted yellow, getting ready to transform.

Snarling, she replies, "No newbie can resist the school!""Maybe I wasn't a newbie...." I don't push the subject. I do NOT want them knowing about my other side.

Sheila yells, "You put father out of work!"I laugh, "Good! He was a greedy bastard anyway!"

Her mouth drops, "You little bitc--"Will interrupts, annoyed and scared at the upcoming fight, "Kate! Stop! I don't see how your complaining is doing anything! The school wasn't that bad, okay!"

His words cut through me like a knife; stabbing me where it hurt most.I take a sharp inhale, glaring at him though feeling my eyes get watery. "You know NOTHING about the school do you?"

He snarls slightly, "I highly doubt it would cause this trouble!" I don't blame him for getting mad, the fire between Sheila and I is putting everyone in danger. He is just looking out for his mate.

My voice crackles, uneasily, "Do you know what they did to us?" I feel my voice drop, remembering the pain. "Do you know how they make you forget you are mythical?"I look up from Will to Sheila and then to the pack. "If you are a vampire, they tie you up to a machine that slowly pierces you with a wooden stake, going deeper and deeper into your skin until you die or loose your vampire side. Usually nobody survived for if you did magically happen to transform human, you would usually bleed out from your wounds. Werewolves..." My tone gets more aggressive, and I snarl remembering the scars I received, "Werewolves are chained down using silver. And as we know, silver burns werewolves, just like wooden stakes hurt vampires. After letting them burn from the silver, they then use silver sticks to poke and pierce you until you turned human, then as a human they would torture you until you turned back into a werewolf; where they would repeat the process."

My mind flashes to the scars I still have on my skin, I growl, "For animal transformers they would also torture your human side until you snapped and went animal. Then they broke your animal. You turn back human, they do it again. And with fairies, don't even get me started!" I snap.

My voice breaks again from pain, "And for those who didn't know what creature they are, they would do all the things to you, even if you were just human. They would stab you, and chain you up. However, the silver chains would be burning to the touch. The wooden stake covered in poison, and ect."

I take a deep breath, noticing the fighting emotions on everyone's faces, "And guess which one I was in?"

Then silence. All were processing the information.Will begins, "k-Kate I'm so sor--"

I shake my head, interrupting, "I wouldn't expect you to understand..."I feel the tears form. No, I can't be comforted. I can't show them anymore of this weakness.

And like the coward I was, I ran. I ran, leaving behind the shocked faces, the pained face of Will, and the smug face of Sheila.

I burst through the house at full speed running right into the forest. But I didn't stop there. My tears were streaming through and my sobs echoed as I ran through the forest. The trees flew by like lightning, though the cold wind from my running did help sooth me. I kept running and running and running until finally, I collapsed. My lungs burned with fire, my legs sore, and my whole body shaking as my tears continued to flow.

I collapsed against a tree. The twilight hour giving its cast of shadow as the last birds sing their songs. A gentle sway of the trees were heard. I just sat there, letting the time past with my head buried between my knees as tears stained my jeans. My mind kept flashing images of the school.

I tense as I feel fingers gently touch my back, right where my scar was located. A deep, smooth voice talks to me, but I am numb, listening, but at the same time not.The voice keeps rambling and rambling. The touch of this person, soothing me as the hand gently rubs my back.

Finally, the voice sighs, "Kate, it's time to go home...."I awaken, realizing it's pitch black outside. I look up to my company, my watery eyes shining against the moon light, "W-what time is it?"

Ethan sighs, removing his hand from my back, and looking down at the ground, "11:30 pm."

I gulp and I nod. Ethan quickly stands up and offers me a hand. I take it with no objection, not noticing how the contact caused my skin to tingle. He leads me back to the house, though I was still numb. My scars were burning up, I knew I needed them to have a cream rubbed on them. Otherwise, they would start messing with my animal side.

I go through the house, getting some looks from the people doing things in various places throughout the house; or looks from the pack.I am gently pulled into Ethan's room; however, am not sent to my own room.

I look up to see Ethan watching me. He shrugs uneasily, "I thought maybe you would like some company tonight?"Though it was more of a statement than question, I still nodded.

The pain burned through me as my scar lighted up in pain. I wince, taking a sharp inhale.Ethan is instantly by my side, putting his hand on my back. I yelp, jumping away.He walks more slowly toward me, causing me to take a step back. He pushes me almost all the way against a wall before looking at me with caring eyes. Gently, he lifts up my shirt leaving me in my bra and jeans.

I blush, looking down as his eyes roam my body, almost hungrily. However, that quickly fades and he carefully rotates me so my back was toward him.

He gasps as he sees the horror of my back and it's scars. I push my head down, moving my hair from my neck to give him a better view. My scar was a long diagonal slash down my back. It was pink, as if it was almost healed. But it never does. Coming from the main pink slash were more scars, that looked like branches coming from a tree. The main scar being the tree and the mini scars being the branches, extending from the branches were smaller scars, in the shape of lighting. So my whole back had this amazing design of scars.

Gently, Ethan roams his fingers across the scar. I gasp as his fingers touch, causing flames to roll through me under his touch. I gulp, taking in the weird sensation that caused my stomach to flip.

He turns my back around, holding my eyes, "D-did the school do this?" He asks pained.I nod my head, looking back down. He sighs, before enveloping me in a hug.This affection I was certainly not used to. I frozen, unsure what to do, before finally giving in and closing my eyes, hugging him back.

He pulls away, as I begin to shake from the pain my scars were pulsing through me. Before long, I am sitting criss-crossed, with my bra off, on his bed. My back was toward him as he put the cream on my scars, instantly numbing the pain.He mumbled something as he finished and turned away so that I can change into my pj's. That I appreciated.

He lead me to his bed, were he insisted that I slept. I had no energy to fight so I did what I was told. He quickly followed me, crawling next it me on his bed, holding my eyes as I began to fall asleep. I said nothing, and I am glad he didn't push it.

My eyes began to close as my body enjoyed him petting my arm and his warmth. Finally, with one last sigh, I was into dream world.

Hey everyone! I know this is an annoying authors note, but I just want to thank you all for the 700 reads! Thanks so much, it really makes me feel good!

And.........

Because this is a short chapter and for all your lovelys who vote (you know who you are), I will be uploading chapter 12 tomorrow night, or 1/23/14.

Please enjoy! ^_^

Chapter 12- Threat

I quietly sat at one of the benches at school. I've avoided most of my pack, not yet willing to answer their questions. I woke up extra early, sneaking away before anyone woke up. Though I did cook them breakfast.

Right when the school opened, I was in a classroom getting tutoring. I was falling behind on my math and science. I slipped into my math classroom and began working on some worksheets, asking the teacher for help.

Not to long after, Ethan popped into the room wanting me. I refused and the poor teacher was pale from fright. I don't see why but I quickly told the teacher I wouldn't let anything happen to him. He relaxed slightly.

I got a pass to my science class and when I entered, the class was taking notes so no talking. Fighting I skipped and the rest of my classes had the same flow.

I was right now at lunch, outside sitting alone as the cool winter breeze ruffled my hair. My ears naturally eavesdropping as I wrote my paper for History.

A voice sneered, "Well well well, such a coward aren't we...."I growl, not looking up from my paper. I really need to finish this and get this b*tch off my back!

"What do you want Sheila?" I say, my hand scribbling an endless flow of words.She snarls, "Stay away from my mate, and my pack!"

I sigh, "Sorry, I'm kinda trapped there." Then hissing, "and you aren't the alpha female or the mate of Ethan!"She slams her hands on my table causing me to glare up at her, "I will be the alpha female and I will tell you what to do!"

I roll my eyes, "Good luck, Princess...."She growls as I continue my paper, ignoring her as she rambles and throws insults at my way. My eyes travel up as a dark shadow reaches my paper.

An older man, in a business suite, smiles politely at me. "Hello. My name is Daniel Howl. I heard you are the new runner of my daughters' pack."

Well hello, Dan.

I nod, "I'm Kate."He smiles at me, chasing his tone to a more darker tone, meant only for me, "Please stop messing with my daughter and her mate, otherwise the consequences will be severe."

Well well well, back to the warnings. He must not know who I am.

I smile back, "Well then, tell your daughter to stop making assumptions she can't prove. Now if you don't mind, I've got better things to do than to act scared and whimper helplessly under your command. So please, excuse me!"

I slam my binder closed picking up my stuff and leaving my shocked father behind. He doesn't control me anymore!

I storm though the hallways, stopping as I felt the familiar buzz of my phone.My eyes skim over the contents, a text. A text from an unfamiliar number. Leave and never return or have yourself and your pack punished.

I roll my eyes slamming my phone back into my pocket and putting my backpack into my locker. I decided to leave my backpack at school, I've got no more homework and that paper is due in two weeks anyway. I shut the locker door closed, turning on my heal.I freeze as I flip around. In front of me stood a well-built handsome male. The boy smirked, tossing his styled brown hair to the side.

"I couldn't help but notice that such a pretty girl is lonely." His deep, rolling voice muses.I roll my eyes, scoffing, "Im fine being lonely, it allows flirters to leave me be!"He growls dangerously his eyes flashing yellow. "You are going to play for that bitch! Nobody talks back to me without my command!" He gives an evil smile, "Maybe I might claim you... Teach your lesson!"

My breath hitches. My eyes quickly scan him, my body tensing as it mentally prepared itself for a fight. He is a werewolf based on the yellow tint in his eyes, and he has a player's charm. No voice sounded that smooth."She's mine!" growls a new voice. Wait, I lied. There is one natural voice that sounds like that. My body tingles as a firm hand wraps around my waist, pulling me into a well-built body.

I'm his? What? My eyes travel to Ethan. However, his attention was focused on the werewolf.

In a blink of a second I am fling gently into a locker, my body getting stuck. "Ethan!" I shout in anger. I could have taken him! Then, my fire melts away allowing fear to flow in. Not in fear for myself, but fear for my....um.. Never mind.

Ethan and the werewolf go into a death hold. Snarling erupts and I watching horror as the two lung at each other. One scratch from a werewolf could kill a vampire unless received the blood of a mate.

I wiggled in the little locker, my legs sticking out awkwardly as my body was jammed into the locker. I had to help Ethan! More groans and grunts sound out, and shrieks of pain.I kept wiggling in worry, trying to get free as the fight became bloodier and bloodier. Both were equal in strength!

My world slows as I watch the claws rack across Ethan's face, meaning the death of him, and a punch sending him flying through the hall and to the outside.

"Ethan!" I squeal out my arms bending the metal around me. I felt the familiar warmth of my animal side giving me strength. Then I felt an icy cold run through my limbs. My scar burned, but it burn with ice.

I froze for a second. My scar did give me a very powerful magic. I never tried to tap in on the magic after that night. But this time, I wasn't in control. I felt my speed and strength double, my weight minimize, and my senses come alive. The ice feeling burned through very part of me, making my body scream in pain, but I had to get to Ethan!

The werewolf gives me a sadistic smile, coming toward me. I jump out of the bent locker as the wolf lunged at me. With any easy push, I slammed him into the locker, causing a dent in the metal. He collapsed onto the floor, loosing conscience as I look down at my hands in surprise. I didn't know my scar gave me that much strength! I barely lifted a finger!

Then another emotion took hold of me and I wasn't in control again. I zoomed outside, papers flying off the walls from my speeds.

In a blink I was leaning over to Ethan. The scratches on his face oozing purple and green. The poison that would kill him.

"Ethan!" I shriek out. I look around. My only chance was to give him blood! I lifted him up with ease. Again surprised at my strength and ran into the cover of the forest. My teeth bite into my skin, causing a steady flow of blood to begin. Ethan mumbles something, his mind lost.

I slam my bleeding fist against his lips, prying them open. He moaned in fear, before realizing what it was, then he moans in pleasure. His fangs grow out and I scream as they pierce my skin deeper, sucking up my blood hungrily. It's like he never had blood before.

My brain gets light-headed as the pain from his bite increases, his hands grappling onto mine to make sure I don't move. My scar numbs the pain, allowing it to make it bearable. Finally I hear him gasp as remove his fangs.

I sigh, a wave of relaxation hitting me as the warmth heals my cut and I fall backward, into his arms. I give him a slight smile, feeling the warmth of my animal side leave me and the power from my scar disappear.

He looks down at me, gently holding me as his face portrays shock, and realization. My eyes shut as my mind whirls, What did he realize?

Chapter 13- Mate

Ethan's p.o.v

I watch as the girl who just saved me passed out in my arms. Her hair falling over as her breathing steadies and slows. Vampires bites have this horrible pain that comes as the skin is pierced. I am very surprised she was awake during it. Usually it caused the person to pass out. However, after the pain came a state of pure bliss, which finally caused her to faint.

I wasn't going to use my poison on her at all; actually. (It's the poison that causes the pain). I was just going to lick up the blood, knowing it probably wouldn't do anything. But when the first drop touch my tongue, my tastebuds exploded with flavor. My vampire took control and I hungrily ate.

Her blood was so delicious. Nothing like I've ever tasted before. It was sweet and tangy but had this fighting feel to it. My body's reaction to her blood was even more surprising. I went full on vampire!

I groan remembering what I wanted to do with her as her wrist slammed into my mouth. Let's just say it was pictured dirty and fun. I was dying and my last thoughts were about bedding her. I'm an idiot. But then again, why did her blood work? Only a mate's blood can heal a werewolf bite/scratch. My fingers skim over my cheek, noticing the cut was gone.

My eyes glance back over to her sleeping figure. She was so calm and peaceful looking. I gently place her down under a bush. She will have to wait.

I felt the buzzes of my pack mates intensify. Right when I step out of the forest I am met with their startled and worried faces.

"Ethan!" cried out Athena, lunging at me for a hug. I embrace her, knowing I have to show emotions. "We were so worried about you bro! We all felt that sting of pain....what happened?" asks Jack.

I sigh, "Some new werewolf attacked me. I haven't eaten real food for over two months, so I wasn't very strong...""Two months!" starts Anna, "Ethan! That isn't good for you!"

I nod my head, "I know. I know... But it's time to get that werewolf, story later."Léo scrunched his nose, "But aren't you weak?"

My tongue instantly goes to my teeth, where some of the blood was still there, causing another explosion of taste. "No, I have just eaten...."Everyo ne shares a confused glance before I roll my eyes, "I got blood, like from a living creature. Don't worry, she isn't dead."

"Wait, she?" asks Will.I sigh, "I'll tell you once we start moving, so can we please start?"The group nods as I take the lead, moving into the school. People quickly parted out of my way. I inwardly grin, I can be that scary when I have to be.

I begin, connecting my whole group through their minds so they can see images too, "Alright so it started with a werewolf gaining up on Kate." My mind flashes that image and it travels to everyone, "then I attacked, getting cut. Kate somehow stopped the crazied werewolf and came to me. She forced me to drink her blood and I tried to control myself...but...but..."

Anna finishes for me, her voice traveling through everyone's head as we got closer to the school's door, "But you couldn't for she tasted too good?"I nod my head, my hand grasping the cold door handle and swinging it open.

The group froze in shock. Papers were everywhere, the locker I jammed Kate into was bent as if the Hulk had pulled it open. The werewolf was slowly standing up, leaning against a bent locker as if someone was slammed into it extremely hard. The tiles from the walls scattered and cracked.The hallway was just a mess!

What happened?

I feel my my anger rise, remembering what the werewolf did. I storm over, my pack closely behind me.The werewolf snarls, standing all the way up. "You are back. I thought I scratched you!"I growl, "You did, but I got my medicine!"

The group perks up slightly, realizing that Kate's blood saved me, and only a mate's blood can save you.The werewolf growls, lunging toward me.

I snap my hand up, freezing him in his tracks. Woah! I look at my hand surprised. This power of mine hadn't showed up since that witch placed a spell on me. Maybe the spell was breaking. I tried to remember the words as I effortlessly lifted up the werewolf, using levitation skills; another power I haven't seen in a while.

Something about a curse or spell being broken by a mates dispell? No that can't be it. But it had something to do with that!

I growl, making my spirit travel over the werewolf and digging inside him. I quickly find his pack, and his alpha. He shrieks out in pain as my dominating spirit digs into him, reaching out to his pack.

"What's going on?" A trembling voice says, probably because it's not used to the call of another alpha.I turn towards Fred, one of the bigger pack's alpha on this territory. The werewolf still levitating in the air behind me. "Fred, as you know there is a no attack policy on school grounds. Your pack member clearly broke the rule by attacking me."

First shock lights up Fred's face, then it darkness. "I'm sorry Alpha Ethan, I won't let it happen again."

I nod my head. Fred has given me plenty of times to show I can trust him. I drop down the werewolf as he gasps for breath. Fred glares daggers at him as he storms out the door, the werewolf trailing behind, sorrowfully. If he had been in wolf-form, his tail would have been between his legs.

I sigh leaning against the lockers, feeling a want to check on Kate.Anna places her gentle hand onto my shoulder, "You want to go check on her?"I nod my head, Kate is taking over my mind!

Anna smiles, "congratulations, my single Pringle, you no longer have to be single."I glance down at the small girl with a wicked smile on her face, "Huh?"

Will chuckles slightly, taking Linda by hand, "You seem to have a mate bond with my sister."

"Wait what!" My mind screamed though I kept a relaxed face on, "what do you mean?" I got way to good at hiding what I really think.

Léo smiles, wrapping his arms around Anna's waist. "Her blood, I'm guessing, was addicting to you. You always want to see her and be with her. You get protective over her, and have that sexual desire. Also, the witch did say your powers would return at the finding of your mate. Giving you her blood did save you. So she must be your mate."

I shake my head, not wanting to take this in yet. Anna nods, "We can all see it Mr.Vampire. You just can't."

This is causing too much of a headache! Kate kept flashing up in my mind. I really wanted to see her! F*ck!

I rake my hand through my hair before leaning my head against the bent locker. I need to think. Kate pops up again in my mind. I groan inwardly as I realize I won't be able to.

The bell rings signaling a new class to start. I push off the locker, turning toward my small, but powerful pack. "Get to class, I need to go."

The group nods before scrambling away. I fell their buzzes numb and I quickly go over to where I last left Kate.She was still there, asleep, and before I realized what I was doing, she was in my bed sleeping peacefully while I was just watching. Thinking.

Yes, I finally could think now that she is in my sight. So she was my mate, does that mean I have to claim her? Would she accept being my mate? Would she make a good alpha female? Will she help me with my powers? Though she can't transform, unlike her sister, she does seem strong enough to be leader. If only she could transform!

I groan running my hands through my hair as I tilt my head back shutting my eyes. This is just too f*cking complicated!

A small moan escapes the lips of my gorgeous mate, "What's the matter, Ethan?" Her sleepy voice asks. I instantly feel my animalistic side purr from her saying my name. I have to admit, I do enjoy hearing it coming out of those full lips.

I feel a stir in my stomach and my mind flashes an image of her on my bed. No Ethan! You have to be gentle about this, or try to be.

She frowns. Her bed hair giving her this sexy, wild vibe. Her soft voice speaks up, "So I saved you with my blood?"

I nod. I could almost see the gears of her mind spinning as she realizes what is going on. Her mouth drops, "You're my mate?!?"

I snigger, "Well runner, what can I say? You are stuck with annoying me until the day you die."

I am fan-girling so bad right now (insert scream here). This book is at 1k reads. 0_0... Thank you everyone so much for the reads and votes! I'm glad everyone enjoys the story. EEEE! ^V^

Anyway, being that I am super excited and very thankful, the next update will be on: 1/27/14

Please enjoy! :D

Chapter 14- Pleasure or Pain

Kate's p.o.v

As soon as I heard those words, my first thought was:F*ck! F*ck! F*ck!Ethan's voice tuts in my head, "Tut, tut, tut, runner. What did I say about cussing?"I groan, "Why the freak did I give him my blood?! Stupid freaking animal side who wanted to save him!"

"That still counts as cussing runner..."

I growl back to him, through my head, "Just because you 'might' be my mate because of my blood, doesn't mean you can control me....or my language!"He smirks, holding my eyes as he responds back, "I also want to know what this 'animal side' that you have is."

I groan again, rolling my eyes, "Just shut up Ethan."He wickedly sneers, leaning his hands against the bottom of the bed, "Now now runner. You don't want to break my heart, right? So you'll tell me, right?"

I grumble under my breath, "I want to rip your heart out," before snapping, "My animal side is the other side that felt the mating bond with you. You stubborn blood-sucking parasite!" My blood pressure rose with my anger.

He flashes his fangs and I feel my eyes try to change. No. Don't you dare. I tell myself, controlling my eyes.

Ethan raises an eyebrow in confusion. I quickly look around the room, noticing I am not in my own. I sigh, quickly getting out of the bed. I stalk toward my room, feeling Ethan's eyes travel my form as I go toward my room.

With a swift swoosh, he is blocking my doorway; leaning against the doorframe, his bare chest showing boldly. He smirks, "Where you going, runner?"

"To change."He flicks his hair away from his eyes all sexy, "We are mates, you can change in front of me." He pauses, "Wait, do you know what are mates are suppose to do to seal the bond right?"

I feel my face heat with a blush and I quickly look down, my eyes wide from surprise and realization. He smirks, "Apparently you do..."

Gross cocky vampire!

"Well, since we aren't mates yet, I do get my privacy!" I try to push Ethan to side, except he became a wall. "Ethan.....move." I growl.

He lifts his hand up, resting it on the top of the door frame, "Sorry, Princess, no can do."

"Ugh!" I groan out, throwing my hands up and storming back into the room.Like a spoiled child I throw myself onto the bed, crossing my arms, and pouting.

Ethan's smirk deepens as he walks over to me. I throw my gaze away, pouting at the wall until I feel him radiating heat on my skin.

"To close! To close!" screams my normal side. My breath staggers as I finally turn toward this hulking beast. O.M.G.His perfectly sculpted chest, stomach, and whole upper body in-general was right in front of my looming eyes. There was a six pack and all his other muscles were well-toned. His muscular arm was leaning on the bedpost, allowing his head to rest on it as his own eyes gazed over my body. His smirk vanished and was replaced with a more emotionless gaze.

I blush deeply as I catch his electrifying blue eyes with my plain brown ones."You don't have plain brown eyes, you have absolutely gorgeous and intriguing hazelnut brown eyes..." Ethan replies in my head. My stomach does a flip. Did he just compliment me? My animal side purrs, wanting to close the space between us. Ugh! Stupid animal side! Why are you making me go all goo-goo eyes for him?!?

I let out a small breath as he lifts himself off the bedpost, and looking down at me. I felt my skin heat up even more as his hand gentle grabs my chin, raising my head.

"Kate..." He whispers, sending shivers down my spine. The way he said my name made my heart want to melt.I gulp, allowing my eyes to catch his. His touch was causing butterflies in my stomach and flames to erupt under my skin.

I whisper out, feeling my mind loose control, "Ethan...."He sighs slightly in pleasure as his name left my lips.

I gentle pull my head out of his hands, allowing my curious eyes to loom over his well-built figure. All his muscles were toned and gorgeous. I cautiously trace my fingers on his stomach, and around his muscles. He shivers under my touch, my animal side purring from making him react.

I pull back, feeling the raging war between my two sides. Then the pain starts.I gasp, feeling the explosion of pain in my stomach. I feel my spirit roar to life and reach out to those around it. I feel myself leave my body, seeing, but not. My spirit instantly feels Ethan's powerful spirit, contracting itself from it, but still staying near. It travels down through my 'pack' until it feels a spirit full of fear.

I blink gasping for air as I return to my world. Ethan holding me by my back, full of worry. "Kate? Kate! Answer me! Are you all right?"

"Athena!" I scream out feeling a stabbing pain slice across my face. I scream clutching my face though no blood was there. The pain vanishes before it takes hold of a new victim; Ethan. He yells as the pain takes him and he doubles over into the ground, rolling on the floor, and gasping in pain.

I find myself at his side, gently petting his bare back. I lick my lips, "I-is Athena h-hurt?

Ethan takes a deep, still shaking from the pain, and nods. "She had just been attacked by demons, but Jack found her."I gasp, before collapsing onto the floor next to Ethan. "It-is she al-live?"Ethan gives me a small smile, "she is a god, demons don't kill her instantly like most of us."

I nod my head as he continues, "she is, however, severely hurt." He mumbles something under his breath.

"Huh?" I ask, pushing for more information. He sighs, "I felt a spirit touch mine before she was attacked... I'm guessing which ever creature was planning to attack had to see if the alpha was nearby.

I shake my head no, scooting slightly over to Ethan to rest my head in his shoulder. My touch caused shivers to go down his back, but he stayed put."I was the one who came in contact with your spirit. My spirit took me through the pack's spirits until it felt one with horrible fear; Athena's."

Ethan jolts slightly, "Your spirit came in contact with the packs, and my own?"I nod my head yawning. My body was again tired. I just woke up but this spirit thing drained my energy; again.

Ethan gives an amused scoff, "Was this your first time feeling spirits?"I nod my head slightly against his shoulder, my eyes closing. I hear him sigh, "We will have to go to witch Esmeralda tomorrow and receive some info on our mate bond....." Then he mumbles, "And figure out this power you have..."

I shuffle, getting comfortable against him. My animal takes over allowing my spirit to roam and feel for Ethan's. He tenses under me as my spirit comes in contact with his. Both spirits purring deeply.

He sighs, gentle moving his hands under me and carrying me back onto the bed. He mumbles, "Get some sleep, you just unlocked a new power, and felt the pain of an alpha..."

I yawn, snuggling into the bedsheets before mumbling, "how about you?"Ethan sighs, his voice melting away, "I feel this a lot...."

Then I disappear. Disappearing back into the dream world where I just came from.

Ethan and Kate getting closer and closer together. Does anyone ship them other than me?

Anyway........

Thanks to everyone who reads!!! I really apperíciate it and I'm glad you guys like the book! The next update you must be wondering? The next update will be on Friday, 1/30/15

Enjoy!

Chapter 15-Attacked

Kate's p.o.v:

When I finally woke up, it was a blur. I was full of energy and needed to throw it off. I quickly found myself outside, jogging laps around the mansion. There was no way I was going back to school. Even if I only had four periods left. I noticed how Athena's spirit was more calm, she must have gotten the medicine.

My chest heaves as I lean against a tree, out of breath. Leaning my head against the rough bark, I enjoy the coolness of the winter air on my face. The forest giving a shadowy overview to the ground.

A smell wafted to me, werewolf.I growl, flipping around to face my stalker.

The handsome boy sneers, his arms crossed in front of his well-built chest a couple trees away from mine. I instantly tense, pulling out my headphones from my ears and dropping them onto the leaf covered floor. I push off the tree to stand back up as I watch the boy closely.

"Not you again!" I snarl. He smirks, untangling his arms and coming closer to me, "Ey, I have a name you know...runner."

I tense even more, hating how he used my nickname. I bear my teeth as he comes closer. I recoil back subconsciously. He flips his dark hair from his eyes, smirking, "I'm Hunter, what your name?"

I quietly judge him in my head, before catching a scent of a werewolf female. Knowing there is only one werewolf female in this school, my lips curl up into a slight smile, though I was glaring daggers.

"Oh you should know, Hunter, what my name is. You work for my sister. What did she do to get you to hunt me? Seduce you?" I snarl as he keeps taking steps forward and I take steps back.Hunter smirks, "No, she just promised me you after she and Mr. Daniel Howl were done with you..."

He was now towering over me, and I was backed up to a tree trunk, trapped. His gaze goes to something behind me, "Ah, Mr. Howl, I have brought what you wanted."

I gasp sharply, smelling the familiar sting of my father's scent."Yes, thank you Hunter, you have done well." I bite my lip, feeling my body tense, ready to run. My animal side just needed to get out, or release some of its energy.No. Don't transform, keep your scent hidden.

Daniel comes over, taking Hunter's place and snatches my chin forcefully into his hand. I growl bearing my fangs. WAIT FANGS?!?

I quickly shut my mouth, hoping no body noticed."Ah, you are the little free-runner who has caused so much trouble to my daughter...."I wanted to scream out at him how he caused it himself by sending me away, but I kept my mouth shut. If he didn't know it would be better.

"Whats your name, free-runner?"Silence.

Hunter scoffs, "Its Kate."A growl emits from Daniel's throat, "Did I ask you?"Hunter quickly pales in fear and looks down, shuffling, "No sir...."

My father nods, "Good boy, now Kate... please explain to me what you are doing with Ethan."Instantly my animal side roars to life, getting protective over my privacy and Ethan. I feel my body give off a scent and I panic slightly inside. However, quickly it is hidden by an overpowering scent. A pack of werewolves in wolf form.

I growl, feeling the warmth of my animal side travel my limbs as it senses danger, "None of your business, DAD!"

I roar slamming my foot into Daniel's groin and dashing away as shock and pain took hold of his face.

Then, I ran. Ran for my life as a pack of wolves, about ten strong, chased me to get to my blood. Their paws hitting the ground echoed behind me as I began to catch speed, just running straight into the dense forest.My hair wiped painfully across my face as I zoomed through the forest, trees passing by so fast you couldn't even see them. My animal side giving me the speed I needed just to be barely ahead of the pack.

I curse mentally as I look back to see two horse sized wolves now joining in this game of tag. Hunter and Daniel were now on my tail too. The forest wiped past me. The cold air painfully numbing my face as my breath started to get uneasy. My breath grew heavy as the wind whipped my hair.

Because I haven't fully transformer I was running out of breath. The wolves howled in joy, their prey almost at their claws. I shrieked slightly and gave myself another burst of speed as a werewolf's jaws came awfully close to my ankle. I just kept running straight straight straight.

"ATHENA!" I scream out as I see my friend in my way.

"WHAT THE F*CK DID YOU DO KATE?!?!" Athena screams as she connects us mentally.

I quickly catch up to her as she starts her own run from the wolves. The wolves howled again in joy, now they have two prey to catch!

"I didn't do anything!" I scream back mentally, panic taking my body as I ran. My legs burning from soreness. "Kate, TURN NOW!" Athena screeched in my head as one of the horse sized wolves made a lunge for my legs.

I turn painfully, slipping on the leaves but quickly being back in the run. The wolves whine out slightly in pain as they crashed into one another but were also back on their feet in seconds.

"Alright Kate, Turn in eight feet and jump onto the second tree on your right. THEN CLIMB FOR YOUR LIFE." Athena yells in my head.

I nod, allowing my animal side to be used more to give me more speed. I burst past Athena, following her instructions perfectly and quickly galloping up into the safety of the tree, the pine needles poking the bare skin on my arms and legs.

Athena was next to me in seconds, panting. I give her a quick nod in recognition and freeze as one of the wolves howl under our tree.

"We lost them! F*ck!" shrieks out Hunter.Daniel growls next to him, pacing around the little forest area. He finally sits down on his haunches as flashes a wolfy grin. His wolf voice echoes around the lively forest as he speaks to the rest of the pack, "We can lure her out with part B. Is everyone in place for part B?"

Another voice speaks out, "yes, we are all but missing the goddess...um.." "Athena," interrupts Hunter, annoyed at loosing his prey.

Athena's eyes widen and she looks at me, her mouth hanging open like a fish. I put a finger to my mouth telling her to be quiet. I go back to the scene below us as the pine needles covered us.

The wolf Daniel shakes his head, "We can still continue as planned. The males of the pack are on a hunting trip correct?"Hunter nods, his shaggy brown fur glistening in the sun as he began to leave the premisses.

He growls, "Come on guys, we need to make sure Sheila has got in positi on."The pack howls and quickly follows Daniel and Hunter away into the forest, leaving me and Athena still hidden in the tree.

"PART B?" She yells out."SSSHHH!" I respond loudly, then whispering, "They are werewolves they might be able to still hear us.."

Athena nods before taking a deep inhale. Her eyes widen in realization as I notice I haven't turned off my animal yet and my scent now being easily smelled."You're a animal transformer?!?" She hisses.

I look down, nodding, "Yes, I had to keep it a secret though."She throws her hands up in the air, perching on the branch only on her legs. Damn she has good balance, "Do you know how many female transformers there are?!? Almost none! Do you know what you could do with the power of being an animal transformer?"

I sigh, nodding, "Yes, but its better to make sure your enemies don't know that..."Athena watches me sternly. I give an uneasy smile, looking away.

Athena and me gasp together as we feel a huge pressure and feeling of fear inside us. We catch each other's eyes as our faces pale. "Linda!" We yell out together finally realizing what Sheila's part is, she was to endanger my new family!

My eyes instantly flash blue in anger almost causing Athena to fall off the branch in surprise. I give an uneasy chuckle, "sorry..."She nods before holding my eyes again, "Wait, how did you feel Linda's feelings?"

Though I didn't want to admit it, I did, "I think from Ethan, being that he might be my mate..."Athena raises an eyebrow as I roll my eyes, "Fine, that he IS my mate."She grins, before going back stern, "Okay so we know the werewolves are going after the females in our pack so they are going to the school right now."

"Yes, but they are ahead of us on the path to school and we need to beat them. But we can't show ourselves! How are we going to do that?!?"

Athena gives me an evil grin as I frown, and thats how I ended up swinging from the trees like a monkey.

Hey everyone! I hope you enjoyed this chapter!

We are getting to the fun part >;3 woop woop!

but anywayyyyy, because the next chapter is going to be a interesting one (hint hint nudge nudge) I need some time to write it. So the next update: 2/3/15

I need time to edit and make it good.

ANWAYYYY ENJOY!

Chapter 16- Animal

E than's p.o.v

We all gasp as we feel the pressure of fear coming from one of our pack mates. Will screams out in pain, his wolf clawing the ground as he screams again.

I quickly rush over placing my hand on his warm fur, "Will! What is it?" Will's horror filled eyes catch mine as he whispers, "Linda...."

-------Kate's p.o.v

I carefully watch the scene that was 50 feet below(I was in a tree). Linda whimpering as Sheila, the pure white wolf, circled her on the field. Fairies could not use their magic inside school unless in magic class so Linda was powerless.

Anna, the leopard, was pinned down by the massive wolf of Hunter. The boys of my pack were nowhere to be seen. Daniel was quietly watching in the shadows as Anna snarled and tried to fight back. The werewolf pack who chased us was surrounding the whole scene. I glare, feeling my scar start to tingle. My eyes were piercing blue as my animal side kept taking over more and more of my body. I don't know what I am, and that was what was scaring me not to jump yet.

Athena whispers next to me, "What's the plan?"I growl as Linda shrieks as Sheila lunges slightly before going back to her circling. Linda was sobbing so loud I could hear her from the large pine tree I was perched in.

"We need to separate the girls from the pack, get them into two groups. I'll take care of the pack."

Athena eyes me, "You sure Kate?" I nod my head, "I know I don't know what I am, but I know I am strong."Athena nods, her eyes traveling back to the scene."When do we attack?"I purse my lips, listening to the scene below.

Daniel scans the trees before finally looking at Sheila, "Break her bones.... we must lure Kate at all costs.""NOW!" I roar out as Sheila tense to attack.

I scream out as I jump off the branch, falling toward the ground. Everyone's eyes snap to my falling figure as I fell to my death.

Wait, WHAT AM I DOING?!! Jumping off a 50 foot tree?!

Sheila lunges grabbing Linda's arm with her sharp teeth as Linda screams in pain. Shelia has an evil smile plastered on her lips as I fell. Athena shouts from above, "KATE YOU IDIOT!"

The ground came closer, and my fear started to rise. My breath became panicky and I couldn't breath from the cold air batting my face.Then, peace took hold of my mind. Instantly my animal took over my body, allowing strength and speed to enter. Then, my scar explodes surrounding my body in an icy feeling. That's when it started.

A weird tingling took over my whole body. My lips grew outward curving into a sharp snout with many fangs. My head was pushed down and stretched out as my legs and arms grew longer, both being the same length and bulging with muscle. My nails grew out to be curled claws. My body stretched out, becoming sleek and narrow as my skin hardened. The tail bone grew out becoming a spiked tail. From my shoulders sprouted two huge wings. They looked like bat wings, bones holding them then flaps of skin in-between. My skin slowly changes in color, becoming silver and transforming into scales. My eyes become sharper and all my senses intensify.

I roar, snapping out my wings as the ground came dangerously close. The wolves whine out in fear at what I have become.

The feel a heat come out of my throat and I open my mouth to release it, flames explode from my mouth, covering the field in an icy blue flame. I gasp, quickly looking down at my giant body. I was a SILVER DRAGON!

I throw my head up, roaring into the sky in happiness. The werewolves quickly scramble away leaving Sheila looking petrified on the field as her snout still held Linda's arm.

I roar again, loving the feeling of the wind through my scales. The freedom, the wind, the speed! It was amazing! I sharply close my wings against myself tilting toward the ground.

The wind whistled as I dived down. I snap them back out to slow down my fall as I land onto the ground with a 'THUMP'!I growl, coming closer to Sheila. She was only a little smaller than me. She was about horse-sized, while I was slightly bigger.

She growls, releasing unconscious Lina from her snout, snarling, "Who are you!?"I growl, beginning to circle her, my long tail allowing me to make tight curves, my body radiated with power, and she felt it. "I'm so surprised you don't recognize me, sister!" I hiss, my forked tongue snaking between my fangs and sharp teeth.She growls, "Likely story!"

My eyes spark slightly as I feel my throat heat again, "You don't have to believe it!"I roar, pouncing over the passed-out body of Linda and ontop of Sheila.

She howls back, attacking me. Her snout closes on my leg. Her teeth slip off my scales, unable to puncture me and I am released. I growl again grabbing her throat between my own teeth and slamming her into the side of the school.

She whimpers out in pain before passing out. My tail swooshes behind me, waiting to make sure she doesn't get back up. I finally notice the crowd around us. I instantly go into defensive mode, circling around the body of Linda; growling dangerously.

Anna gallops over, her leopard body allowing her to quickly come near. A wolf whines and I instantly snap my body around toward the sound, allowing Anna to tend to Linda. The wolf takes a step closer, clearly in worry.

I growl, snapping my teeth and the wolf takes a step back. I don't trust wolves just yet. His front two paws pawing at the ground in worry. He runs around and I follow him until he stops next three amazing other creatures.

There was a massive lion with silky black hair, Léo, the wolf, which I am now guessing is Will. Then there was two absolutely gorgeous mythical creatures. A powerful horse stood on the left. It's skin a greenish-blue and its wild hair that was pure water. The water mane billowed behind it as if it really was hair. I growl, feeling my icy flames in my throat. The horse neighs and throws it head back, keeping its distance.

My eyes travel to the right. In-front of me stood a handsome raven-scaled beast, another dragon. It's pitch black scales giving it a radiant vide. The purple eyes gave contrast to the dragons powerful body. I snarl, noticing how me and is other dragon were complete opposites, even though this other dragon is slightly bigger than me.

We both tense and flash our fangs, with our tails swooshing behind us.

I roar spreading my wings to the sides. The dragon in-front of my takes a step back, confusion spreading through its eyes before anger takes over him again. I look at my wings quickly and take my own little step back in surprise. Both my wings had my exact scar design!

The dragon opens his own wings, roaring, a sign that the fight is about to begin.Athena yells from across the field, finally getting off the tree. She was panting and stopped both of us, "ETHAN! KATE! Don't fight each other!" She screams.

The dragon's and my eyes catch. Ethan speaks in my head, surprise flickering over his dragon features, "Kate?"

Well fuck...

Hey everyone! I hope you enjoyed this interesting chapter. It took a lot of time, and personally, there were some plots twists that I wasn't even expecting, but hey, once I write..... my imagination takes over.

Anyway, I would love it if you guys comment, but thanks for reading! It means a lot!

Next update: 2/7/15

Chapter 17-
Blood-Sucking Bastard

than's p.o.v

Kate? I accidentally say in Kate's head through my bond. Oops. She'll be very confused when I come home.I hold my ground in shock, my eyes traveling the sleek body of this creature. My claws extended into the soil, holding me in place. Another dragon? How could this be? Why did Athena call this dragon Kate? Kate is at home!

I gulp, feeling Jack next to me. He throws his head back with a whine, stomping his hoofs, "Who is this!" neighs Jack in our heads. "Another dragon! Probably wanting this territory! Ethan you have to fight it! Make it go away!"

I feel Anna connect with us, "No! The dragon saved Linda you idiots!!!"I growl, "are you sure?"Anna's narrow tail begins to swoosh in annoyance, "Yes! There was a figure that jumped off the tree with Athena and turned into this dragon!"

I shiver as I feel two more spirits connect, one was dominant while the other was just following along. I shiver slightly from the new connection but not noticing how one of these I've never connected with before. I was too angry for this dragon being a secret!

I flash my teeth at this stranger dragon, warning it. "How did we have a dragon on our territory a secret?!? Or is he new student?"

Athena shakes her head, "you idiot! All you males are idiots! That dragon is not a male!" We all freeze slightly, looking closer at this dragon. The dragon was sleeker than me, more shinny, more feminine.

I growl, ignore the messages my dragon side was sending me, "Ya? Prove it!"

Athena comes up to the dragon, placing her hand gentle on its neck. The silver dragon shivers, not used to contact. She whispers in all our heads, "come on Kate, tell them."

The silver dragon shakes its head, whining while lowering its head in embarrassment. Athena growls dangerously, "Kate, you can hear our whole conversation! Just show something!"

"I can't Athena! What will they think?" Kate's voice echoes in our heads. What?

How is Kate connected? My black scales shiver as this dragon's icy blue eyes catch mine. I take a step closer to this silver dragon, feeling my power radiate off my scales. The dragon takes a step back, fear flooding its eyes. However, it didn't back down, it stood its ground.

I whisper, "Kate?"

The silver dragon looks at me with shock, holding my eyes. It takes a step forward. The dragon was defiantly feminine, by the way she moved. The silver dragoness' blue eyes held my own. I shiver slightly, noticing my scales making themselves become more vibrant.

What are you doing body?! She isn't our mate!

I watch the dragon carefully before I hear Kate's sweet voice echo in my head, "Ethan?"

I sigh, connecting only with the female dragon and blocking everyone else out, "Kate is that you?"

The dragoness nods, looking down, embarrassed. My mate is a dragon! What the heck?

I take a step forward and instantly Kate rears back, spreading open her 15 foot sky blue wings in defense. She snarls, flashing her fangs. I'm guessing she hasn't done this very often, but how did she hide her scent?My eyes gaze over the exact replicas of her scar that was on her wings. Maybe her scar was giving her that power? I highly doubt she is a royal.

I take a step back, lowering my head in sign of peace. Kate lowers her wings slightly. I watch as they shimmer against the light as if they were made of crystals or ice. She truly was a gorgeous dragon.

Finally I let my dragon out. "Mate! Mate! Mate!" he yips happily.

I feel the familiar urge of claiming take over my senses. I shake my head, now is not the time!But f*ck, did she look sexy in her dragon form.

I growl slightly, trying to hold back my urges. I see Kate tense her wings back up from my growling. I hear some murmurs around us and I notice the crowd that has surrounded us. Kate's eyes widen and she quickly snaps close her gorgeous wings against her tight body. Her head snaps back and forth before she swivels on her paws, turning toward the crowd.

Then she dashes. She easily turns on her tail, jumping upward over the crowds' heads as they gasp, scream, or yell out. Then she is gone, like lightning she took off.

"Get her!" Screams my animal side. I growl, connecting myself with my pack, "Get everyone back in school, I've got Kate."My pack nods, running off and herding everyone back.

Closing my eyes, I concentrate in the sweet scent Kate. My strong dragon senses mixed with vampire made me have a clear path in my head to Kate.

I growl, lunging forward, dashing after this free-runner. My sleek body easily dodging the trees. This dragoness hasn't had practice in her body much, so she was very slow; and afraid to test herself.

The trees wipe pass me as I follow the sweet scent. Finally, I am able to hear her pacing. I crouch down on all fours, feeling the moist ground under my claws. My black scales easily blending with the forest below.

She paces back and forth in this small open area, looking stressed. I quietly creep around the bushes, trying to get to the perfect place to attack.

Kate lifts her head up and stares at the bushes, that's when I lung.

---------Kate's p.o.v

I yelp as a powerful body crashes into mine, making us both slip. I growl, jumping back up on all fours, "Go away!" I roar, my voice sounding weird. I scoot back slightly, afraid of what I can do.The black male tilts his head amused, "you are such a youngling."

I hiss, crouching low to the ground in defense as the male begins to circle me, "I'm guessing you haven't played with your dragon side too much have you, runner?"

My eyes spark slightly as he mentions my name. Right, this dragon is Ethan."Go away Ethan!" I growl. He sits down, flashing his many rows of sharp teeth, "The last thing you want after a transformation is to be left alone"

I snarl, raising my wings slightly, "then I'll leave!"I jump flapping my wings awkwardly before collapsing back onto the floor with a 'oof'.

Ethan chuckles, circling my fallen body. I give a low growl as I stand back up. "Back to the house runner." He says, power leaking like acid from his voice."Never!" I hiss, tensing my muscles and pushing off into a run.

Not even going a few feet, a body slams into me, pinning me down, "ETHAN! Let me go!" I yelp, squirming under his claws. Dragon claws can hitch onto dragon scales, so no slipping away.The pressure gets stronger and I feel the tingling of my scales where Ethan was holding me down. No, no, no! Ethan don't get lusty on me!

I snarl in fear, adding strength from my animal side, pushing away Ethan and crawling back up painfully before jumping into a run.Quickly I hear his footsteps traveling behind me, as his dominant alpha traits spring to life. I squeal, swiveling to the side.He yelps out in pain as he crashes into a tree. I couldn't help but smirk as I ran faster, loving this feeling of power.

I feel a burst of energy as the mansion comes to view. I yip with happiness as it gets closer and closer until I could jump up onto the balcony. With an easy push, I balancing gracefully on the balcony rails. I cautiously place one paw down on the cold balcony floor before quickly scurrying into the room and into my own. The lock shut and I was partially safe.

I sigh, smiling, that I just got away from a freaking lusty dragon! I shut my eyes, concentrating on having my strength and speed disappear. I slow down my breaths, than heart, then body. After some time, a tingling feeling creeps through my body and I find myself naked on my floor.

I blush deeply, happily thanking that I didn't transform back earlier. Locking my door, I walk over to my bathroom, turning on the hot water for a shower.Quietly, I step in, the water releasing any tension or stress that was built in my sore muscles.

I moan in pleasure, just standing in the warm water allowing the dirt and dust slip off me. I screech, jumping out of the water, as the warm water viciously disappears. I yelp as my foot slips on the tiled floor, my body landing with a hard thump on the floor.

I groan, scrunching up as pain explodes through my back and head. "Kate?" asks an amused voice outside my room. I groan again, slowly picking up my aching body, "Go away!!!"

The person outside my room snickers, "Come on my clumsy runner, get out..."I groan again, slipping on my underwear, shorts, bra, and t-shirt. My hair was still soaking and sticking to my stinging back. I slowly pry open the door to find Ethan leaning against the door frame, smirking.

"What do you want?" I glare at him, strutting past. His smirk deepens, "I wanted you in the house and you said no. I told you to get out of the shower, you said no. But look! In both times you finally listened!" He grins, "So if I tell you what I want, will you listen?"

I roll my eyes, walking over to my closet, "first of all, I didn't hear you! And....You are the one who turned off the hot water, bastard!" I turn towards the closet in rage; however, freezing as I feel a breath only my shoulder. "And that's another thing you do!" I snap, turning to face him, only to find him towering over me.

He takes a step forward, and I take a step back, and repeat, "You like to just sneak up on me and it's annoying because it's.....its," I was now pinned up against the wall by Ethan, my breath staggers.

"Kate...." He mumbles."What?""Shut up..."

My mouth drops, "EXCUSE ME?!? Now why would I now WANT to shut up?"Ethan squeezes his eyes shut, groaning. "F*ck Kate!" He slams his arms to the sides of me, holding me between him. "Because you are f*cking turning me on!" He snaps his eyes open, allowing me to get a glimpse of the lust and want hidden in those eyes.

My mouth quickly snaps shut as I finally notice the budge that was rubbing against my inner thigh. I blush deeply, my body tensing; preparing to run if needed.Ethan growls, putting his head down though keeping me in between his arms, "Don't even try, you'll only turn me on more."

I relax slightly, watching his face in slight fear. God, he was sexy.

Really Kate? When he might go all lover boy on you, you find him only sexy?!?

"Ugh, Kate! Why do you have to be so god damn sexy with all your sass?" He groans, placing his head on my shoulder as he moves his body a little away from mine.

I freeze, unsure of what to do. Licking my lips, I gently bring my hand up, petting his head slightly. He shivers under my touch, enjoying it, before moving one of his hands around my hip and the other behind my neck. Sparks light up and I feel my animal side stir. I stay there a few more seconds, feeling the weird tingling and tightness of my lungs from his touch. I bite my tongue, trying to control myself.

All of a sudden, he protectively pulls me toward his body. I yelp out, now being pinned completely against him. My animal side purring happily. He finally sighs, lifting his head off my shoulder, "I'm sorry Kate. My dragon side went all goo-goo eyes for you and I couldn't control myself."

I give a slight smile, feeling me warm up, "It's fine....." I relax in his arms, feeling quite comfortable. My animal side was acting up, wanting us to take it a step forward. But I was content with just sparks flying from his touch; for now."Why are you so goddamn beautiful?" He asks. Butterflies light my stomach, and my breath gets heavy.

I stammer, blushing deeply, "I-I-I d-don..."Ethan lunges for a kiss, his soft lips meeting mine. I gasp in slight shock, giving Ethan's tongue entrance it so desperately desired. My body lights on fire and I loose consciousness. I push myself against Ethan as he holds me close, fire lighting up my skin. My hands possessively intertwine in his hair, pushing him closer. It felt sooo good!!

He roams my mouth expertly as I moan out in pleasure. His hands move, grasping my face gently and pushing it to the side; giving his tongue more leverage. Our tongues fight for dominance but eventually his wins as I melt into bliss.

He breaks the kiss, leaving me panting. He smirks, "So... I'm a still a bastard?"I give a slight smile. My body still warm from the kiss, I pant, "Oh yes, a big blood-sucking bastard.

He smiles before have me lunge at him, enveloping both of us into a blissful kiss.

Chapter 18- Morning Tease

I snuggle in closer to my warm wall. My blissful night leaving me tense free and happy. Wait a second. A warm wall?

My eyes snap open, finding me face to face with the 'bastard' from last night; Ethan. I give a slight gasp and tense. Ethan growls slightly, tensing himself in his sleeping self. His arms wrapped around me, holding me near him.

I give a quiet whine in fear as I am imprisoned in his warm arms. What HAPPENED last night?

Ethan lets out a low groan, "You really don't remember?"

I furrow my eyebrows, "remember what?"

Ethan sighed slightly, his eyes still closed and his arm not wanting to loose its grip on me, "I'm reading your thoughts Kate...... And that you don't remember last night."

Well f*ck!

I shuffle uncomfortably, "um....w-what d-did happen?"

Ethan groans, "Shush, I'm sleeping....."

Ya sure you are.....

My body pushes against his hands keeping me prisoner and tries to pry them open. A growl rumbles from Ethan's chest as he pushes me into him. "Eek!" I yelp as I get gently crushed into his chest.

He groans again, "your not going to let me sleep unless you crawl away, am I right?"

I purse my lips. He sighs, snapping open his electrifying blue eyes. I gasp, jumping away slightly. He gives a sleepy smirk, "you really don't remember, do you?"

I shake my head, "Im not sure what you are talking about."

He grins, closing his eyes again, "Well let's see." He pauses, opening his eyes back up to hold mine, "you kissed me, then we cuddled, watched some hunger games.....then somehow, I was falling asleep and you got me too bite you again."

I blink a few times, before abruptly sitting up, this time, Ethan let me go, "I gave you my blood?!?!" I ask, shocked.

Ethan smirked, "What can I say, I'm irresistible."

I scrunch up my nose, "more like disgusting. And why would I do that?!"

Ethan shrugged, his eyes closing, "you said you wanted to feel a bite, without having the feeling of a mate pull or being endangered."

I groan, thinking to myself, "how can I have been such an idiot!"

Ethan smirks, propping himself onto his elbow. I growl slightly, noticing Ethan still holding me,"Ethan....let go of me."

He flashes his fangs, "Now why would I do that?"

"Or I will kick you!" I huff, squirming to get away.

"Sure you will...." He smirks.

I lift up my leg and snap it down, kicking him in his thigh.

He hisses in pain, grasping his leg. I hold back a giggle and jump out of the bed, happily running away, "Told you vampire!"

"Kate...." He growls. I flip around, a smirk on my own face, as I place my hands on my hips, "What?"

He wasn't on the bed anymore.

My eyes widen slightly. Freak!

Ethan's voice echoes in my head, "Tsk tsk...what did I say about cussing?"

I growl, responding back as my eyes scan the room for him, "I can cuss when I want!"

Ethan chuckles in my head, "Yes, just like your allowed to kick me...."

I yelp as I feel Ethan grab my waist and pull me into him.

I squirm, his arms holding me against his bare chest, "Ethan!"

He whispers into my ear, "Gotcha Runner."

He leans down kissing my neck slowly, as I feel myself get heated, "E-ethan?"

He keeps kissing, stopping at his bite, "Maybe I should bite you again, just to see how you respond."

My eyes widen again then get set into a glare, "Don't you DARE!"

I feel my scar give me power and I begin to squirm with more power. I feel Ethan grin on my neck, "I knew you couldn't keep away from your dragon that long runner."

I growl again, feeling his dragon come to life inside him. With a roar I give into my transformation. I pry through his arms as the transformation finishes.

I hiss, my beautiful dragon body crouching a few feet away from the now dragon Ethan.

His deep voice rolls through my head,"You seem to be having difficultly keeping your dragon under control....."

I growl, though feeling my dragon side keep trying to lung onto Ethan.

He circles around me, his tail running down my scales, "oh runner, you can't keep away from me....."

I tilt my head slightly, "maybe not you, but your dragon.... Yes."

I pounce, knocking the black dragon off his feet. I yelp as my feet loose their own ground and I collapse onto Ethan. He grins, his purple eyes flashing as now I am on top of him.

He whispers, "Told you."

"KNOCK KNOCK KNOCK!" Sounds the door as Anna yells, "come on love birds! We got to go talk with Esmeralda, remember?"

I blush deeply, quickly rolling off Ethan. I watch him smirk as he rolls himself upright, watching me gallop over to the door.

With my fangs I am able to turn open the door handle and let Anna in. She smirks, taking in my dragon form and Ethan's, "Alright lover birds, well.....dragons, when you are done playing around you can meet us in the kitchen." She wiggles her eyebrows at me, grinning. My mouth drops slightly and I shake my head, disgusted, "Nope nope nope.....never going to happen!"

She laughs, "We shall see Kate, we shall see...." She winks before turning on her heel and walking away.

I feel a hot breath on my neck. I shiver, my scales rattling.

Ethan whispers, "As Anna said, 'we shall see'."

I growl, turning and slipping under Ethan's neck, "Ya, you probably just dream about it all time."

He turns, also following me, "Which guy wouldn't dream about finally, completing process of mating?"

"Ew!" I screech, "okay, I'm done!" He smirks, letting me storm to my room.

I slam my door shut with my long tail, mumbling, "disgusting dragon vampire boy thingy."

Ethan shouts on the other side, "I heard that runner!"

I groan, settling down on my bed. I close my eyes, trying to concentrate on making my dragon leave me. A knock brings be back to reality, "Runner! You done yet?"

I shout back, "Done with what?"

"Um, transforming?" Ethan asks.

I look down at my body, it was still dragon, "No! It's only been 5 minutes though!"

Ethan gives a slight chuckle, "Kate, it has been 30 minutes."

As fast as lighting I bound to the door, swinging it open with my mouth.

He looks over my dragon body and sniggers, "I see you haven't mastered your dragon body yet?"

I growl, "It's my third time ever transforming, WHAT DO YOU THINK?"

He smirks, "Would you like me to help you? I promise I won't look once you go back human"

His eyes get a mischievous spark and I hiss, "Liar!"

He rolls his eyes, "Kate, you need someone to help you, you won't be able to alone."

"I did last time!" I roar, my tail swinging side to side.

Ethan sighs, "by time three, you need to be taught how to. I'll take you to dragon school as soon as possible to get you at least some minimal training. But you still need my help."

A growl rumbles through my chest as I nod my head uneasily, allowing Ethan through with a glare.

My dragon happily sings, "Mate! Mate! Mate!"

I know she was happy with this,

Slowly, I lay down on my bed, my head resting on my paws as my tail curls around my body.

Ethan begins to mumble something and I shut my eyes, feeling the tingling of transformation.

I bite my lip, really hoping Ethan wasn't watching. But of course, which guy can resist?

I squeeze my eyes shut as a whoosh sounds through and I feel myself go human.

"Kate, you can open your eyes." Ethan says.

I shake my head, "No! I'll see your eyes roaming and I'll get too embarrassed!"

Ethan chuckles, "Kate, you are covered with a towel."

My eyes snap open as I notice the slight pressure on the whole of my body; a towel.

"W-when did you put this on?" I ask, my voice taking a higher pitch.

Ethan shrugs, "When you were still a dragon."

I close my eyes, taking a deep breath before finally letting out, "Thank you...."

"I'll leave now, get dressed. We are leaving in five minutes." Ethan says, walking out. As soon as I hear the door close I jump from under the towel, rushing over to my drawer and pulling out some jeans and t-shirt

I change quickly, being downstairs in less than three minutes. Anna grins mischievously, "You seem happy."

I groan, "don't start thinking that dirty please!"

She flashes me a dirty smirk. I sigh, rolling my eyes though a smile played on my lips, "I'm happy because I beat Ethan downstairs."

Athena laughs from ontop of the stairs, coming down, "Ya, sure you are."

I grin as I watch my friend slip into the kitchen.

Anna smiles, "We got to go Athena, talk to you in three days!"

I give Athena a quick hug before exiting the house with Anna by my side.

My mouth drops into a smile as in the drive way stood a gorgeous lime-green Lamborghini.

"Holy fudge," I gasp as my eyes roam the beautiful car.

Anna grins, "Our parents like to get us presents, let's just say."

"This is yours?" I gasp.

Anna shrugs, "Not exactly, Léo's parents got it for him. But he has another car. He let us borrow this one. Especially that you don't have one. But your records say that you do have a drivers license so……"

I blink a few times before squealing excitedly, "I get to drive?!?"

Anna laughs slightly, "You betcha babe."

I bite my bottom lip, holding back another squeal.

"Catch!" Shouts a male voice. I flip around, just having enough time to have my reflexes take over as that I catch a pair of shiny keys.

I smile, "Thanks Léo."

He gives a wink, "Sure, just don't kill my mate, alright?"

I laugh, "Deal."

I slip into the car, starting up the engine. I sigh in pleasure as I hear the engine purring under my hand. So much power!

A mustang screeches at a stop next to my car. The window rolls down and Ethan smirks, "I see you are ready to go, ey runner?"

I grin, "You betcha."

Ethan presses onto the pedal shooting his car forward onto the road, I grin, quickly following.

"Let's start this road trip!" Anna squeals happily as the car speeds up, purring under my touch.

I grin, as I scan the instructions Ethan sent me telepathically, "I think, for once, I am going to enjoy a trip across a desert."

Hey guys! I know, early update, but this is for my good friend @ashely_hayes64 for she got me to post sooner! Please tell me what you think and again, THANK YOU FOR YOU READS

Anywho, next update: 2/13/15

Chapter 19- Eclipse

I sigh, the peace of the desert settling into my bones. Anna was peacefully snoozing next to me as we were speeding 90 miles per hours across the desert road.

My eyes focused on the road ahead. I haven't driven in such a long time. I sigh again, loving the feeling of power and freedom. It reminded me of being a dragon.

"Enjoying the car, runner?" The only other awake person asks mentally.

I grin, "Of course, who doesn't like a car who can beat you?"Ethan's chuckle sounds through my head, "Is that a challenge, runner?""You betcha vampire," I smirk back, my grip on the steering wheel tightening.

"Fine, your on. 3, 2, 1....GO!" The mustang next to me roars to life, zooming forward."You ready?" I ask the car. As if it could understand me it purrs louder. I grin, my foot pressing harder on the gas pedal.

"VROOM!" My car jolts forward, catching up and passing Ethan's car easily. I look back to Ethan's cars, where he was concentrating deeply on passing me.I flash a wink and speed up even more. Slowly the desert becomes forest as me and Ethan continue our race. Each of us taking turns being first and last.

My world slows as my eyes catch a herd of deer at the edge of the forest, blind to my car."Anna! OUT!" I scream as ice and heat explode through my limbs. My foot smashes the door as I pull Anna out, throwing her out of the car. She screeches as she lands gentle 20 feet away. My hands grab my head for protection as my car screeches into the deer, flipping. Then, my world disappeared. I was in darkness, all to be heard was a voice shouting somewhere, my adrenaline leaving me as fast as lightning. I numbly pry open my eyes.

A gorgeous black dragon stood in front of me. His wings were open and on fire. His stomach glowed orange as he stood confidently in-front of me."He looks kinda like a lunar eclipse...." were my last thoughts as the fear and pain of the car crash takes me into dream world.

-------Sometime later------I yawn, lifting myself out of the surprisingly comfortable bed."Good morning Kate!" A stranger voice pipes up.I instantly bolt, my whole body tensing and preparing for attack.

The melodic voice laughs. Her voice sending pleasant shivers down my spine, "Calm down Kate, I won't hurt you."I finally scan the room, it was just a small cabin looking house. I keep scanning before landing on a gorgeous small woman. She wasn't gorgeous like: be jealous or a sexy gorgeous; she was just........breath-taking. She had lively grey eyes, completely frizzy/poofy light brown hair, and a smile that lit up the room. Small wrinkles around her eyes showed age as her eyes sparkled with wisdom.

"Let me introduce myself, my name is Esmeralda."I blink a few times, "The witch Esmeralda?"She nods before laughing at my face's reaction, "I'm guessing you believed me to be a old green hag?"

I instantly blush, that was exactly what I thought she'd be. Her laugh echoes across the room, causing a smile to play on my lips.

She smiles at me, "I may be old darling, but I am defiantly not a hag." I blush again, turning scarlet, "I'm sorry madam."

"Now now child! Please do not call me that!' Ethan's voice shouts from outside the door, "Kate! you're awake!" I freeze, clutching the blanket covering me. The witch Esmeralda purses her lips before mumbling something. Ethan instantly yelps before grumbling, "Not fair!"

Esmeralda sighs, "Ethan, I know you've found your mate now that your powers are back, but you are not allowed to spy! We don't want to bring up the past darling."

He groans, "FINE!" I scrunch up my nose, "The past? What's wrong with the past?" Esmeralda gives a slight smile at me, sitting down at the edge of my bed, "Nothing you need to worry about child."

I sit up more, still clutching the blanket, "Well if it involves Ethan's than I should know! I'm his mate! I have to know!" Esmeralda's eyes widen, "You are his mate?" I lick my lips before nodding, "Yes," my voice got smaller, "That's why we came here...." I felt like Esmeralda was a loving grandmother and I did wrong.

She gives a slight smile, "Well, that's something I just learned." Ethan's voice echoes in my head, "DON'T TELL HER ABOUT THE MATE THING!" I sigh, before responding mentally back, "Too late"

I lick my lips, "So what is the other reason that we here?" Esmeralda scans me, " Athena...""WHAT! WHATS WRONG WITH ATHENA?" I instantly bolt standing up, leaving my blanket and leaving me naked. I blush deeply, collapsing back onto the bed and hiding myself with the blanket again.

Esmeralda smiles, "You'll defiantly make a great Alpha female. Athena was attacked by demon, though she still is a god, she still is suffering. I'm making her a potion to heal her. All she has now is short term medicines, this spell I am creating will cure her."I nod though still blushing, allowing my hair to fall over my eyes as I lean forward.Esmeralda gasps,"Who did this!"Her fingers skim over my scar and I gasp, sitting back up as I felt the scar flare up under her touch.

I blush again, knowing I couldn't escape as she watched with curiously, "The night of my escape I went to the woods and then li--....""KATE?!? Are you okay?" I hear Anna shout from the other side of the door.Esmeralda smiles gently, "Come on, get ready. We can talk more once we go get materials from the forest."

She snaps her fingers and disappears. Anna rushes in with Ethan and Will trailing behind her. I gasp covering myself up more.Anna laughs, "Why are you doing that Kate? You are clothed!"I look down and blink a few times. How did she do that?!?

Anna smiles putting her hand on my leg as I lower the blanket, "How you feeling Kate?"I shake my head, confused as heck as Esmerelda randomly appears at my doorway, smiling."Um, I'm doing great!" I quickly stammer," Um! You know what! I need a run through the forest." I jump out of bed, rushing past the confused faces.I stop at Ethan, glaring at him, "And DON'T follow me, PLEASE!"

I rush through, quickly finding the door of the cabin as stepping outside.The cold fresh air hit me quickly and I sigh in pleasure. A melodic voice sounds behind me, "Ready?"

I nod, sighing as Esmeralda comes to view."Come...." She mentions me to follow her as we begin on the path through the forest.

Slowly, the seconds became minutes, the minutes hours, the day into night. And I? I was lost in my thoughts as we walked silently through the forest.

I was brought back, noticing quickly how it was pitch black outside as Esmeralda says, "We're here..."

My eyes scan the gorgeous area as my mouth falls open. It was a crystal clear lake, little woodland creatures scurrying around it as fall leaves fell peacefully. The full moon as casting its glare, lighting the open arena with a beautiful blue glow.

"It's gorgeous," I breath out.Esmeralda flashes a smile, "I know child, now come."We settle down next to a willow tree near the crystal lake. "You see child, Ethan was a special little boy. He was born on a lunar eclipse, in 1699."

My mouth drops, "He's that OLD?!?"She chuckles, "In vampire age he is about 18-19 years old. Now, because he was born on a lunar eclipse he was born with tremendous powers. He took both his mother's and father's sides. He was born a dragon vampire. However, being that he was born into royalty, he was a very spoiled child. He had all the power in the world, and no one could tell him 'no'. Well, that power starting changing him. In less than a hundred years he was a tremendous murderer. He would terrorize villages killing all who stood in his way. By the time he was done with a village, everybody was dead, and the village burned to ashes. His own parents lost control of him in that point. He was stronger than both the royals combined!"

Esmeralda sighs, "It was a sad time, and I was still a youngling. My mentor, however, was an old wise witch. The royal parents quickly came to her for her help. My mentor saw a demon growing inside of Ethan and quickly took measures to release him. She cast a spell or curse, whichever way you see it, that took away most of his powers until he found a mate. Once he found his mate, his powers would slowly starting coming back, his mate leading him through the process and controlling him."

"Ethan was released from his demon self once that happened. However, many still feared him. To make sure he would change, his parents sent him off to a beautiful forest area. Beaches and mountains included. There were no humans or villages anywhere near the place. All the powerful parents of the mythical world came together. It was decided that Ethan would own a pack. A pack of spoiled, bored, or need changing royal children. The most powerful children of the mythical world. Many feared that this would cause a power struggle and be the end of the children. However, it did the opposite. It children bonded, Ethan became the gentle powerful alpha, and the pack extremely powerful. With their 6 or 7 selves, they equal the strength of a pack with a thousand members. Ethan quickly built up an empire from this little place. Collecting the most powerful packs across the land. He was the top alpha, he would protect those under him. Even if he wasn't their alpha; exactly. "

She pauses and looks over the lake, "Ethan's powers are returning and I am seeing the hunger come back. His mate needs to be with him completely as soon as possible."

"So there is not a very big chance that you can change the mate thing between me and him?" I ask.She sighs, "Mates are suppose to be the perfect other halves, sometimes, a person has two, but that is very rare."I nod, looking down.Esmeralda smiles, "Now child, you still have a chance if you really don't want him.""You see, there's the thing, I'm not 18 years old yet......."Esmeralda's wise eyes widen, "You're not 18 yet? You do know that you won't be able to feel the full power of a mate's pull until then, right child?"

I shrug, "Not really, I've lived as a free-runner the past five years. I just know I'm his mate because when I gave him my blood, it healed him.""I see....."

Esmeralda responds, deep in thought. "Well, anyway, come this way child. It's a solar eclipse this afternoon and a beautiful flower shall bloom. It's a flower we need for Athena's potion."

I nod, getting up and following her to the edge of the lake. I watched as the moon began to cover the sun, the moon becoming a deep black as the sun's light disappeared and only could be seen silver around the edge of the moon. I look down at the ground and gasp. Popping through the ground a beautiful purple blue flower was growing, it's petals looked like crystals as it shines under the sliver glow of the solar eclipse.

Then a pain took hold of my body. My scream echoed through the forest as I collapsed onto the ground, my body shriveling up with pain as it felt like flames were eating me alive. A white glow surrounded me as I felt my transformation be pushed on me. Instead of tingling it was needles. My skin felt like it was on fire as needles were pushing into me. The ball of light covered me, taking hold of my body as I scream one last time.

"Oof...." I collapse on the ground, the pain leaving as quickly as it came. I groan, standing up on my four paws. I was back into dragon form. Esmer alda gapes at me, "You are a solar eclipse dragon!"

"Hmm?" I ask her, complete confused. I felt the same. Esmeralda smiles, "go look into the water." I padded over and roar in surprise as my eyes landed on my dragon body. My silver scales glowed blue. My eyes were silver white with streaks of blue and hints of black. I was sleeker and my wings were a blue that faded into black. The lightning looking scars on my wings flashed blue as if they were real. On my right shoulder was a beautiful image of a solar eclipse. I shivered, my scales glowing more vibrantly. "Woah...." I breathed out as Esmeralda came to stand by me. She put her hand on my scales, smiling, "I believe you are the only match for Ethan, darling child."

I hear footsteps behind me I turn around around. There, in front of me, stood the black dragon of Ethan; or my mate. However, he looked different. His scaled were still black, but they glowed orange. His wings were a black that faded into an orange-red. His purple eyes had streaks of black with hints of red and yellow. On his left shoulder was an image of a lunar eclipse.

Esmeralda stays back at the lake as I take a step closer; hypnotized to this dragon. All of a sudden I just wanted to be with him, be his, him."You are the perfect match...." She whispers as we come closer. I felt Ethan's warm breath on my head and I finally look up. Our vibrant eyes caught and I gasped. He was.......

"You're a solar eclipse dragon?" His deep voice rumbles."I, uh, Ya. Though I have no idea what that means...." I respond truthfully, looking down.Ethan smiles, "It's alright love, you are still as gorgeous as I first saw you,"The solar eclipse passes as quickly as it came and I feel a tingling sensation as my body returned into normal. The butterflies were still swarming in my stomach as I felt light-headed.

Ethan and I were left in human form, just staring into our eyes. His electrifying blue eyes held my eyes with such intensity I could just melt.In a blink, his lips smash into mine. My eyes shut and I push myself against him.

His teeth graze my lip, teasing me. I moan slightly, my hands intertwining into his hair to push him closer to me. I feel him smile as his tongue takes the entrance. Ethan groans against me as his hand goes through my hair and his other at the back of my neck. He lifts me up as my legs wrap around him. His tongue roams around my mouth expertly as I moan. His body responds quickly by pushing me closer. He breaks the kiss for air.

He places his forehead on mine, smiling, "Sorry runner, you are mine."I pant, my own smile playing on my lips, "Apparently I am, blood-sucker.

Hey everyone! Sorry for the late update!!!

Anyway, I hope you enjoyed this chapter and I can promise you that the next one won't be so lovey dovey and will definatly have so action! Sorry for the spoiler XD

Thanks for the readers and the next update: 2/19/15

Chapter 20- Kidnapped

"**B**OOM!" My fist slams into the punching bag, vibrating the room. I watch the bag as it swings around its hook. Panting, my eyes followed the movement of bag as I was raging furious. How COULD they! I let out a roar as my anger gets the best of me and my fist flies toward the bag."PWOOSH!" The bag explodes under my hand, millions of little white circles explode outward, landing with the ripped bag on the floor. My breath was ragged as I watched what was left of bag. My eyes set in an ice cold glare as my hands clutched into fists.

"Anger management much?" A voice scoffed.I turn to my left, my eyes scanning the face between the bars. I hiss out, bearing my fangs as my body stayed tense; and angry.

Hunter, the werewolf I fought to save Linda and the one who cut Ethan, rolls his eyes, "Look, you can't keep this up."I scream, slamming my fist into one of the bars, "I'm not telling that b*tch anything!"

Hunter takes a step back as I grasp the bars of my little prison, my breath still raged and my fangs still showing. Yes, I was in Daniel's pack house. Though it was more like I was kidnapped and sent to the dungeon in Daniel's pack house.

Hunter sighs, "Ya, you will... He's your father for Pete's sake!""HE IS NOT MY FATHER!" I roar, shaking the bars of my prison room. Hunter takes another step back as tiny pieces of the roof fall off.Growling, Hunter steps back to me, "If you keep this up you'll kill us both from the roof!"Though my eyes shined with hatred, I give grin, "Good! I don't like you anyway!"Hunter rolls his eyes again, before just observing me. I was stripped of all my clothing except my sport's bra and short shorts.

I throw my arms up in annoyance, walking away from the bars and closer to the stone walls of my room, "What is up with everyone staring at me when they come and check on me!"

Hunter smirks, coming closer to the bars, "Maybe you are just that sexy.....""I growl, keeping my back to him and my eyes down.

He sighs, as I feel his eyes roaming my scar, "I can't believe Mythical School did that too you."I lift my head up before abruptly turning and slamming my hands against the bars again, "DANIEL did this to me!" I scream, feeling my eyes change to silver.

Hunter takes a step back in fear, before smirking, "They weren't lying when they said you had fire, I never knew it meant this much fire."I hiss again, my hands squeezing the bars. There was a creak as the metal started twisting in my fingers.

Hunter sighs, pressing a button near my jail. I screech out in pain as electricity travels through the bars and into me."Kate, calm down. Seriously, they are just going to test your strength."

I glare at him, backing away from the bars and sitting against the cold back wall, "By strength you mean my power, my animal. Also they are going to do tests on me to see what I have, how different things effect it, how emotions effect it, and other fun dissections!" I bend my knees, resting my arms and head on them as the cold of the wall began to settle into my bones.

Hunter grabs the bar, looking at me sorrowfully, "No Kate. It won't be like that."I snap my head up, screaming, "REALLY? Then why is EVERYONE talking about it? This freaking pack is messed up!"

Hunter purses his lips, not wanting to go deeper into the conversation.I mumble, "Out of the frying pan and back to the dissection table."Hunter sighs, "Come on Kate, try to calm down. You need your energy for tomorrow."

I hiss, speeding into the bars and slamming my hand against them. The roof shook as I snarled, "Make me!"

Hunter holds my eyes for a second before signing, "With pleasure......" From his pocket he pulls out a needle. I take a step back. There was no way they are putting that onto me!

"Good, now if you behave I won't use this." Hunter smirks.I growl, settling down on the floor. My fantasies allowing me to wander to scratching off those pretty little features off his perfect face with my nails then throwing his body into a pool of acid, with man-eating sharks that had razors instead of teeth.

My arms hang loosely on my knees as I scan the room for something to punch. I growl, looking away, "Give me another bag.""No no no runner. What's the magic word?" Hunter teases.

He did not just use that nickname! That's Ethan's nickname to me!What!? Kate! Why are you still thinking about him? He was the one who betrayed you!

I growl again, standing up. My fantasies becoming more and more bloodier as I walk over to one of the walls.

Hunter's smirk instantly drops, "Kate...... Don't even think about it!"I flash a grin before reeling back my arm and slamming it into the wall. The whole place shook as my fist left a pretty big dent in the wall.

"F*ck Kate!" Hunter curses as he opens the door and throws in the punching bag. "You are going to take this place down!" He yells, panicking almost.

I give a hateful smile before hooking up the bag where the old punching bag hung. "I did ask....." I point out, happily.

Hunter grumbles something under his breath."Din Din!" A voice sounds. I walk over to the bars, my hands holding them tightly as I glared at the person that decided to walk down the dungeon stairs to see me.

One of Daniel's pack members walk down the stairs and place the food down at my feet. "Eat it sugar, you've got a big day tomorrow and we can't have you all weak now!"

I hiss at this girl. She had sly green-grey eyes and blonde hair. Too perfect, too sleezy.I roar out, slamming my fist into the punching bag to prove I wasn't doing anything they told me to do.

The girl, named Jazzy sighs before smiling brightly at me, "Come on! Eat up!"She pushes the plate under my door. I stare at the plate. It looks absolutely delicious. The aroma drifted into my nose and I bit my lip, trying to keep from eating it.

Jazzy smiles, before turning to Hunter, "we put a herb in there that she cannot resist. She is an animal transformer, and a powerful dragon. So this herb will give her lots of energy, and it will also put her to sleep."

My eyes turn back to silver and become slits as I roar, kicking over the plate of food.I hold Jazzy's eyes with such spite she staggers before mumbling, "Was not expecting that."Then her smile vanishes, "Kate, time to take you down......" She mumbles something, then it starts.

I scream as I feel a stabbing pain travel through my body. Jazzy was smiling sadistically, as I collapse onto the floor screaming in agony as the pain shriveled up my body. "Make it stop!" I scream as hot tears rolled down my faces as I was rolling on the floor.

Jazzy smiles before turning on her heel as the pain still held me prisoner, "That should hold her!" She happily sings before skipping out of the dungeon.My screams echo the dungeons as the pain felt like it was ripping me apart. Hunter was getting paler and paler from my screams before he too left because of my screams of agony. Before long, darkness takes over. My body passes out as all I felt and saw was darkness and pain.

"There, because it put her to sleep, she'll be strong tomorrow...." A gruff voice says.My eyes pry open just barely as my breath was ragged and painful. My eyes closed again as now the pain was numb now, but my energy down to zero.

Hunter's pained voice rings out, "Is her skin suppose to be doing that?""Doing what?" The gruff voice, Daniel, asks."Flashing to silver scales and back to skin and repeat?"

Daniel, or my so called father, smirks, "It's part of her transformation. She'll make an amazing weapon once we break her. Watch over her tonight, no taking your eyes off!""Yes sir," mumbles Hunter sadly.

I listen as Daniel's footsteps disappear before opening my eyes some more.I choke out, "Why?"Hunter purses his lips, leaning his muscular arms against the bar and watching me."Why did you do it?" Hot tears stain my cheek as I feel the pain start up again. My body collapses and my eyes fully shut as the pain returned.

Quick flashes of today's events go through my mind. Leaving Esmeralda's, Ethan looking weird as we got out of a car, Ethan frozen as Daniel's were-wolf pack attacks, Ethan mumbling, as if he was a robot, something and getting money as I am chained up. Anna and Will gone and Ethan driving off as I am dragged away, crying and screaming my heart out.

The nightmare realm finally takes me as my last thought stood out in my mind, "Did Ethan really do this? And if not, will he come back?"

Chapter 21- Escape

"Up n attem runner!" A deep voice sounds.I lift my head up. A cold glare set on my features as I remained silent; just sitting in the darker parts of my tiny room.

A handsome figure smirks, leaning against the bars, watching me, as Hunter runs in behind. After Jazzy's little treatment, she got rid of all my anger and hate. So, it was replaced with the second best thing: annoyance.

Hunter sighs, "Kate, this is Prince Pierce, the soon to be vampire King."I scoff, looking away, "Ya, whatever."

The handsome, tall male grins, "Cocky..... That's for sure."I roll my eyes, turning my body around so my back was facing them.Hunter quickly stammers, "Actually Jazzy just took out her anger and hate."

The dark haired boy with sky blue eyes smirks, "I'll put a spell to cancel that out as long as she is here."Hunter scoffs, "If you want her to kill you by bringing down the roof, be me guest."Pierce's voice rings out, "Runner, turn this way."

I keep my back turned."NOW!""Ugh....." I sigh like a hormonal teenager and turn around, my eyes holding those of Pierce.

He raises an eyebrow, before smirking. I gasp as my anger and hate pound into me. My scream echoes in the corridor as the power I received from the hatred returned rapidly.

I super-speed to the bars, slamming my hand against them. They rattled under my impact as I scream, "STOP IT!"Pierce takes a step back in surprise before coming right up to my face, smirking, "Make me...."

I roar out as more of the taken power pours in, causing my scar to burn with the want of making mc transform. I stumble back, grasping my head as it all pours into me. I collapsing against the wall before a new wave hit.I scream out, slamming my fist into the wall. The whole room stutters and shakes as both Pierce and Hunter take a step back in fear at what my punch can do.

I pant out, feeling a new wave of pain coming, "Make it stop or I make this place come down!"Pierce smirks, lifting his hands up in surrender. Though the pain was still there it was bearable. "I'll make a deal with you Kate, transform and come with us and I'll make it painless."

I growl, flashing my already transformed teeth, "So that's what this was, a trap!" My voice yells out from anger as I stand up and slam back down into the ground. There was a huge dent on the stone floor of my prison where my body collided; as if I was the hulk.

Pushing my hair back, I glare at the two well-built boys, "Deal." Surprise flashes across Hunter's face as Pierce sneers.Instantly cold takes over my limbs and in a blink my transformation was finished.

I can't help but smirk as the two gaze on my body full of awe. After the solar eclipse, I grew to a huge size. I was bigger than a full-grown horse, my wingspan stretching to be about 18 feet. My silver eyes were piercing silver with streaks of blue and my scales still glowed. I flash my sharp pearly fangs, "Finish your part...."

Pierce shakes his head, leaving the daze, before grinning, "Told you I'll break her....."Instantly I feel my emotions return and I turn back human. Crossing my arms I give the boys a confused look, "What?" I ask as they stare at me shell-shocked.

"You're a dragon and can transform with your cloths still on?!?!" Hunter shrieks.I groan before sticking out my wrists in my cell,"Are you going to take me in, or not?"

Pierce sighs, unlocking my cell and clicking the hand-cuffs onto my wrists, "Off to Daniel's we go."

------------Few minutes later--------"Enough!" I yell out catching the attention of all the bickering adults and teens here. I look down at my cuffs before rolling my eyes and pushing away my hands from one another. "SNAP!" Sounds the cuffs as I rip them apart as easy as if they were a dry stick.

I smirk at the faces of surprise that travel across the room, "Now, before I make this fight of you guys against each other, to become a fight against me, please tell me why you want me in dragon form?"Daniel growls from behind his desk, all the scientists in white-coats still too afraid to speak, "We have a deal with a.....very powerful enemy of yours. We need your weakness."I purse my lips, before leaning, "I see. But why am I needed?"

A female scientist perks up, "You are one of the most powerful mythicals, finishing your weakness finds almost everyone's."I nod my head slowly, "Alright, so now that I got the information I need. Let the fight begin!"I flash a flirty grin to Pierce and Hunter and snap my fingers."WHOOSH!" All the lights go out and the room becomes pitch black.I roar as the yells of fear from scientists become intensified and as my transformation finishes. My eyes instantly adjust to find Hunter and Daniel in wolf form, and Pierce's vampire features come to view. I flash a smirk before taking a bow, "Bye..."

My front paws lift up and slam down. The floor instantly turns to ice as I bolt for the door and my enemies slipping on the ice. Woah! I haven't seen these powers before!I yelp as I slip myself and crash through the door, sliding down the hall and stopping at a new gorgeous beast.

A mixture of relief and hate burst through me as I see Ethan standing there, fire burning around him as ice grew around me.

He hisses, his wings open to the sides, "What are you doing here!"I yelp as I try to stand back up but slip again.He sighs, touching his snout to my neck to try to pick me up. I roar in pain, jumping onto my feet as he burned me.My anger wins, "WATCH IT! And WHAT AM I DOING HERE?!? What are you doing here? You sold me to freaking them!"Ethan snarls, "What are you talking about, you sold ME to them!"

A voice shrills with laughter, "So silly, if you both sold each other and drove off, that could only mean one thing, either both of you drove away. Which can't be true, or...... Or that both of you got kidnapped and a very smart witch cast a spell on you!"

My head snaps to the left to find Jazzy smiling sadistically there. I roar, "SHUT UP!" My wings snap out and I push them down, causing a wind that knocks Jazzy down. I watch in pleasure as her smile turns into horror as ice from the floor crawls, as quickly as fire, onto her, covering her up.

I gasp as I feel my mind being free and what really happened coming back to me; all the bad memories forgotten."Kate, look out!" Ethan yells, running toward me.

I scream as I feel werewolf teeth lock onto my back leg, pulling me down. My body collapses onto the floor with a hard thump. Ethan whines, coming close to the ice, and about to jump onto it."No! Wait there!" I yell mentally to Ethan I as am dragged away. He stops at the edge ice covered floor. I flash a grin, winking. He furrows his eye brows in confusion.

I give a fake whine, "Oh no! Please stop! Please hold me by my back scales, and defiantly not my wings. It'll hurt too much if you bite of my soft delicate weak wings!!!" I give a fake cry, "Please please please don't!"

The wolf of Daniel growls happily under me, letting go of my leg as jumping to get my wings. My world goes into slow motion as my scar flashes as if it was really lighting and shoots electricity toward Daniel's mouth, right before his snout snaps shut around the delicate wing.

He yelps out in pain, being electrocuted into the opposite wall. I painful get back up, my leg bleeding where he bit me. How did you manage to bite me?

"Kate! Let's go!" Yells Ethan already running down the stairs as the scientists in the room I left where slowly starting to get back up with anger. I close my eyes, concentrating on Jazzy and the ice melts away. I grab her cold limp body in my jaws as I feel the memory of Ethan selling me come back. Sorry Jazzy, I already got the memory of what really happen in here.

My dragon body allows me to follow Ethan with ease as we run through the house and burst through the front doors. Ethan transforms right there and runs to the nearest mustang. "We'll steal this...."

He quickly begins to high-jack one of the cars as I put Jazzy into the backseat and freeze her again. I transform and take my seat in the front. Ethan mumbles as he finishes starting up the car without the keys, "Won't freezing her, kill her?" He slams into the gas petal as shouts of protest get closer. "Nope. I don't know my powers yet, but they seem pretty cool. Though, I trust my dragon side enough to know that if she says she won't die, she won't die. Now come on, we got to get to Will and Anna." I reply cheerfully.

Ethan gives a quick nod, driving to the place where me and him where hidden and Will and Anna put into sleep.

Hey Everyone! Reptile here, I was just wondering if maybe you can comment on what you think I should do next and what you think of the book so far? I'm having difficulty continuing :/.........

Annyyywaayyy, Next update: 3/2/15

Chapter 22- Demontic Fight

My breath was ragged as I faced the vampire and werewolf in front of me. My fists were bloody from the little fight I just had with another werewolf type creature from Daniel's little pack.

Pierce smirked, easily walking around me, "I see Ethan hasn't marked you yet, what a shame...... Especially if I could do it." He disappears using vampire speed. I flinch slightly, knowing that the game became slightly more dangerous.

I growl at the werewolf still in my vision, "Why do the demons want me so badly?"

Hunter scoffs, "Why would I tell you that, Princess?"

Pierces sickening laugh echoes around the forest, "Tell her wolfy, she'll be dead anyway."

I snarl, still circling Hunter as our eyes look on each other's. Ethan took Anna, Will, and Jazzy to Esmerelda's because, as he said it, 'he could fly and it would be faster'. Instead he left me with these fools and a half demon half werewolf thing which disappeared after I killed it; apparently.

Hunter watches me carefully before lunging. My foot kicks out, hitting him in the side. His perfect balance topples as I grab his arm, flipping him down onto the hard ground.

Pierce's voice comes deadly close to my ear, whispering, "Tell her wolfy."

My arm snaps back, but hitting air.

"Missed me, dragon!" Pierce sneers, his voice being everywhere again.

Hunter wobbles up to his feet, his blood leaking from his nose, "Well start at the basics shall we?"

He lunges toward me, but I easily duck his fist, landing my own one on his face. Stumbling back he continues, "Demons want to control the world. They already do that to humans using horror and horror movies. Humans are foolish creatures that can't see evil when it's right in front of their nose. Politics were a game set up by demons and so was money. But anyway," he roars, grabbing my slender body between his muscular arms before tackling me to the ground.

I scream as I feel my rib crack under the pressure. My legs lift up to my chest and slam into his body. He flies off of me and into a nearby tree. I stumble upward, clutching my broken bone. My eyes shot daggers to Hunter as he also stood back up.

"There are three types of demon. The shadows which are distractions....."

I feel a cold breath on my neck and I whip around, slamming my foot into the invisible body near me. I hear a small grunt of pain before the whoosh of super speed. I whisper with a smirk, "Gotcha, vampire."

I laugh with hate, "Distractions like Pierce!"

Pierce's chuckle sounds around us as Hunter goes back into his fighting position. "There are the possesy, which posses people who may be opened up to evil."

I attack, using my shoulder to hit Hunter in the gut, making him fall to the ground. He groans as his back smashes into the floor. His strong hand grabs my ankle, pulling me down into the ground also.

I hiss as pain explodes through my back and head. Nimbly, I jump onto my feet; however, he was already on his feet. His fist slams into my face causing a new explosion of pain to travel through me. I stagger back seeing black dots in my vision.

I duck as his arms aims for me again. I grasp the arm with two hands, twisting as I bring my body weight down to bring him down. I feel warmth travel through my limbs and I get a wicked smile, "Continue......"

His breath was heavy, and his heart rate fast as he staggers onto his feet one last time. His face clearly bloody and the body not much better, "This third type of demon is your worst nightmare. It can transform into anything, be anything, but usually likes to be in a dark form. They are all ruled by the same thing, we think, but that's enough information out of me."

I hiss feeling my eyes turn blue. My body slams into his with super speed and strength knocking us both into a tree. I clutch Hunter by throat, slowly dragging him up until his feet barely touched the ground, "tell me, NOW!" I scream. This is no longer a game.

Hunter gasps, his eyes bulging and his hands tried to claw at mine. "SPEAK!" I yell.

"Let him go. And it's the demon king," a smooth voice sounds behind me. I hold onto Hunter a few seconds longer before dropping him like the rag he is.

"Get out of my sight!" I hiss as he rubs his sore throat. He pales before scurrying off. I flip around, my fangs showing and my claws extended.

My eyes travel from the form of Ethan, Pierce, and Hunter who were now side-by- side.Oh my god, it's a freaking strip show here! Help me now.

The three guys in front of me were truly sexy, but I was too angry to notice that they looked like freaking models.

Pierce smirks, not taking his eyes off me, "See you in a week brother...." Pierce disappears as fast as lightning, taking Hunter and leaving Ethan.

I could tell Ethan was having difficultly to find the right words. Too much lust, fear, and worry was in those gorgeous blue eyes.

His eyes roam my body hungrily as I ask, "Brother?"

He shakes his head, shutting his eyes. His voice sounded strangled as he responds weakly, "Pierce is my brother. All the pack's families are coming into the house in one week...."

I raise an eyebrow before placing my hands on my bare hips. I literally had a bra on and booty shorts. The fight stripped me of my clothing. What is up with Daniel's pack and my clothing?

I smirk, noticing how hard Ethan was trying to be mad. His worry and lust, however, got the best of him.

I shuffle over, before standing right next to him. "Ethan....." I whisper waiting for his eyes to open.

His eyes stay snapped shut as he gives a low growl, "What Kate?"

I smirk, "You know I was wondering why you and Pierce looked so sexy, then I realized you guys are from the same mother!"

Ethan's angry eyes snap open, "WHY DO YOU THINK PIERCE IS SE---"

I lunge at him, catching his lips with mine hungrily. His hands intertwine with my hair, pushing me closer to him. I give a slight moan as he teasingly nibbled at my lip. I opened my lips, giving the entrance to Ethan's tongue as it so desperately desired.

"Come on love birds! We got to get going!" screamed the now healthy Anna. Looks like Esmerelda was able to save them.

I smiled as we broke the kiss. I hold Ethan's eyes before sneering, "Jealous?"

Ethan let out a sigh before smiling, "Yes, and you have no idea how badly you scared me when I felt your pain." He eyes watch me intently, "And apparently you still have some."

I finally realize the pain in my ribs. I give a small smile, "I'll be fine, lets go."

Ethan snakes his arm around my hips, helping me walk to the car as my mind took in the information about the reality of demons. They were no longer a fairytale for little kids, they were the war.

Chapter 23- Done with Sass

I hiss in pain as the car stops suddenly. The seatbelt against my broken rib not helping the pain . Yes, I heal very fast, but broken bones usually take a day or two.

I look around the small town from the car window, "Where are we?"

"We are in Forestbreeze, a small town in-between my and Daniel's, or your father's, territory." Ethan responds, putting the car shift onto park.

I furrow my eyebrows, "Why are we here?"

Ethan sighs, "Remember when I told you in a week the parents are coming?"I mumble, "and in a week is when I decide if I want to stay or not....."Ethan purses his lips before continuing,"Well it's a mascaracd ball, and you need a dress. The best dress maker in the world lives here, so we are coming here."

Dress maker?!? I need a dress?!? Since when was I attending this dinner?!?"Anna! Will! Wakey wakey!" I shout, twisting to look at the back seat to change the topic.Anna and Will instantly bolt up from sleeping on each other, slamming their heads together. I snigger as the two rub their heads in pain as scowls were plastered on their faces.

"What was that for?" Anna asks, half-asleep. I grin, "we are in...." I pause, scanning my brain for the town we are in."Forestbreeze," Ethan answers for me.

Anna's eyes snap open, "Ooooooo!!! Are we going dress buying?!?" She squeals.Ethan smirks, looking back, "You betcha tiger."As fast as lightning Anna bolts out of the car door as I just blink a few times trying to figure out what just happened.

Ethan sneers, "It's called being a girl sugar,""It's called being a girl sugar," I mouth out sarcastically as I slip out of the car.

It was a small town in the middle of a forest. Little old one story buildings with little restaurants and shops. Almost as if it was for 'insiders only'.

I sigh as I scrim over our lunch place. A little hole-in-the-wall fast food place called Henry's Hamburgers.Ethan leads the way into the small restaurant. I have to admit, the inside was better than the outside. It was a peaceful little place with diners all enjoying their meals. As soon as our two boys step into the little restaurant, all the girls turn toward their direction.

I feel something stir inside my stomach as each and every female eye-raped Ethan and Will. I scoff, looking away as I cross my arms.

Ethan smirks in a whisper, meant only for my ears, "Jealous, runner?" Three female waitresses come up to our little group, instantly flirting with the two boys.

I cough, "You wish!" My eyes, however, watch the girls closely. How they batter their eye lashes. Secretly unbutton some buttons to show more cleavage or even walk with a more sexual stride. It's disgusting!

The girls latch onto Ethan and Will as we are lead to our table. Ethan and Will sit down on one side of the booth while Anna and me on the other. The girls giggle, trying to seductivly say, "A waiter will see you soon," but with no success.

I see Anna snigger as her eyes notice the girls starting a mini-fight to see who would wait on our table. I raise an eyebrow watching them. Eventually, a skinny, big-breasted blonde came up to us. Her skirt two sizes too small and her blouse stretching across her breasts painfully. The other waitresses stood not to far behind.

"So what would you like today big boys?" The blonde asks, bringing her body forward so her tight blouse was right in-front of Will's and Ethan's eyes.

Time ticks on and the blonde just didn't leave. She eventually opened her blouse slightly to reveal what was there. She leaned over the boys and showed so much it was just....Bleh!

The blonde waitress winks, "Your food will be right out babe...."Anna and I flinch, both feeling the weird lust vibrating from our two males. Did she just forget about us?!? I know, I'm more worried about not getting food than the girl trying to steal my mate. But still!

I growl, abruptly standing up. The whole diner turns to look at me. Instantly all the waitresses eye my body with disgust. My hair was a mess and I was in a brown ripped leather jacket with a white t-shirt and some ripped jeans(that was all Esmeralda had). The blonde snarled, "What do you want? We don't serve sluts!"

My mouth drops before I scoff, "Okay! I know I'm not the cleanest woman here. But I can assure I am a woman! I do not like being disrespected. Whether it be you ignoring me and my friend completely, or just those looks of disgust!" I snarl, slamming my hands on the table, "I didn't freaking just come from a fight to be treating like this! You want the two boys that are my company, take them!!! But don't you start fucking with me!"

The blonde takes a step back before smirking, "In restaurant policy you are not allowed to harm an employee so please leave this premises......slut!"E than looks up at me shocked as I just stood, completely tense. My tongue runs circles in my mouth as I nod my head, "Alright, alright, you want me to be a slut. I'll be a f*cking slut!"

I rip off my itchy leather jacket, showing my bleeding arms. Everyone in the diner was now curious and completely in a mix of awe and surprise at my scars. I rip off the white t-shirt, revealing my sports-bra and black and blue bruised stomach with the broken rib. The crowd gasps as I snarl at the blonde, "Your turn slut....."

I slip out of the booth, walking confidently out of the restaurant. I slam the door shut behind me before taking a deep breath, relaxing my nerves before the sound of the door opening brought me back to the earth.

Anna grins as her arm hooks through mine, "You go girl!" I give a small smile, "Do you know any other places to eat? Ones without bratty waitresses?"

"In-fact I do! Though it's a bar, the people are more chill....."I nod my head, slipping on the t-shirt though leaving the jacket off, "Let's go..."

Anna leads me through the small town until coming up to a little bar. It was literally a door in a brick wall; talk about hole-in-the-wall. Inside it was all dark, but it still looked like a high quality bar; surprisingly.

I got up to the waitress, "A table for two please....."The waitress smiles, "Sure! Please follow me!"

Yay! She's not a brat! She is getting an extra tip from me!We are lead to a small table and handed two menus. Before long a young man comes up to us and we order burgers.

I sip quietly my sprite as my eyes roam the dance floor. Couples were actually dancing!A strong smell of cologne hits my nose and my head instantly snaps to the left. There a handsome, very muscular man walks by us with a grace not seen in humans. As he passes by, a phone falls out of his pocket.

My hand grabs the small thing before looking up at Anna. She shrugs, mouthing, "Werewolf."I nod my head before following after the guy to give him his phone."Hi, I just wanted to let you know--" I begin."Don't bother. I only date skinny girls and truthfully, I am quite out of your league!" He says, waving me off as if I was trash.

My jaw drops. The nerve of this guy was amazing! I sarcastically answer, "Fine by me; I don't date shallow douchebags. Anyway, I just wanted to give you your dropped item."I drop the phone into his hand over-exaggeratedly as his friends from the other table snicker.

I begin my walk back to my table before flipping around on my heel. I snarl, "By the way, you are not in my league; you are just below it!"If I thought he couldn't get any redder, I was mistaken. His friends blew up in laughter and I could see steam out of his ears.

He growls, coming dangerously close to me, whispering, "You don't know who you are messing with little girl...."I smirk, "Oh I think I do...."

The man tenses as a silver knife presses against the lower part of his stomach. I allow my eyes to flash blue then back to brown as the guy stumbles back surprised.

He mumbles curses as he turns away, walking toward his hollering friends. I turn my head toward Anna, "Thank you very much, my lady!" She smiles brightly at me, "It was a pleasure, madam!"

We giggle as we walk gracefully back to our seats, the food was already placed down so we hungrily ate.

A familiar voice rings behind me, "So this is where you ran off to...."I give a low growl, "Where else to go? All the other place had was slutty waitresses. This place actually has men! Even if they are douchebags."

Ethan gives a low chuckle behind me as Will pulls in two chairs into our table.Anna glares at Ethan and Will. With her mouth full, she asks, "Why did it take you so long?"Will turns bright red as Ethan gave an uneasy chuckle, his hand scratching the back of his head.I sneer, "They enjoyed those waitresses giving lap dances to them."

Will turns even more red as Ethan looks to me, sneering, "Jealous runner?"I roll my eyes, leaning against the back of my chair and scowling, "Please! Why would I be jealous of those women?"

Ethan smirks, "Not jealous one bit?"I shake my head. "Nope!" I say, popping the 'p'.

Ethan's smirk deepens as Anna shoves another piece of burger into her mouth. "So when they coming?" Anna gurgles through her mouth full of food.

"About...." Ethan checks his phone, "About thirty minutes...."Ann a squeals, quickly swallowing the food like a snake, "This is so exciting!" She shakes my arm as I plaster a fake smile, "The best thing ever!" I respond.She squeals louder.

Help me now.

Hey everyone! Sorry for the such long wait for this post >~<. I was recently really busy with school and didn't have time (or the energy ;( ) To post. Well, now I will try to post more frequently!

Again sorry for such a long wait!

Oh, and if you guys can check out my newest story, that'd be great. It kinda has the same flow as this one. I promise, that in both the stories I will update frequently. Thanks guys!

Next update: 3/24/15

Chapter 24- Alleyway

I groan as Anna pulls me into a alleyway.

"Anna! I am not putting up with those two seeing me half-naked! Or Léo or Jack! You guys go dress shopping, they are out!"

Anna groans, "Come on Kate! It's a tradition!"

"Tradition. Tradition?!?! Why is the guys seeing you half naked while you try on dresses TRADITION? Wouldn't you want to surprise your mate with your beauty?"

Anna purses her lips, "I guess you are right, but then you have to convince them!"

I sneer, "To chicken to do it?"

Anna gives a fake scoff, "Naw honey! I'm just too beautiful!" She does a hair flick, grinning wildly.

"I like beautiful. Usually means more weak!" A gruff voice says.

Anna and I flip around at the same time. A little gang blocked our exit. An old man in front followed by a bunch of gangster teen boys.

I finally scan where Anna took us, "Really Anna? Into a freaking brick alleyway! Don't ever let me listen to you again!" I joke.

The older man snarls, "Why you laughing? This might end up the end of your life! Defiantly your virginity. "

I raise an eyebrow, acting like these boys were not there. "Anna, why are their so many icky people in this town?"

Anna shrugs, still looking at me, and playing along, "Well this town is know for the most murders and rapes of young girls. People say a gang called Sticky Fingers do all the crimes though they can never catch them."

I raise an eyebrow as I place my hands on my hip and look at the approaching group, "Sticky Fingers? Really?"

The older man grins wickedly, "Yes you got us babe, you can called me Middle. Middle Finger."

I snort, feeling Anna pale as their group kept flowing and flowing in with teen boys, "funny, but want to know what my name is?"

"Hmm?" Middle asks, grinning as he cornered us in.

My eyes flash blue, "Death......"

I roar, ramming into the man and taking him down swiftly. I unclip the knife from his shoe before feeling three bodies fall ontop of me. I grunt as one lands on my broken rib before slamming my elbow into the stomach of one. Like dominoes, they pile off of me, giving me room to assess the scene.

Anna was in leopard form attacking some frightened humans as I noticed one that was mumbling to himself. This boy was trying too hard to stay hidden, and sweating too much for not fighting; however, he seemed too young to be in this gang.

I slip into the fighting mass of boys. Being that they are teen boys, their hormones are not to balanced. One punch can lead to the whole group fighting against themselves. That's exactly what happened. The boys were now fighting each other, other than me and Anna.

My stride doesn't stagger as I walk over the fighting bodies until I stop behind the mumbling boy. I smirk, before whispering into his ear, "Caught you, cutie."

The boy yelps, flipping around. His fearful look only lasted a second before my fist rammed into his chest, sending him flying.

Instantly, a large amount of boys disappear, though the human boys were still fighting, not noticing the weird change.

I grin, "Clones.... Nice touch. Especially how you changed their hair color, eye color, and size. Though, not changing the shape of the face kinda gives it away."

A glint enters the boys eyes as I kneel down, holding his green eyes gently. He looked about 10-12 years old. "You are a young, but strong magic wielder. What are you doing with these thugs?"

His fearful eyes jump from fighting body to fighting body behind me. The chaos not slowing down but Anna doing exceptionally well. This 10-12 year old hasn't been in a fight before.

He was a child.

Oh you poor thing.

I gently put my hand to his cheek. "What happened?"

Wow, from fighting to helping children.

His eyes dart to Middle as he slowly stirred. I sigh before mumbling, "Rape, murder, and the torture of little kids."

I glare at the boy as I stand up, "If you make the clones come up, you will be severely hurt. See that person over there," I point to the rising figure of Middle. "If he hurts you, I can hurt you ten times worse. I know what you are. You are a Mythical, like me." The boy's eyes get a sparkle in them, "But if you stay, I will protect you with my life and take you away from here...."

I slam my fist into a teen boy behind me, causing him to pass-out. The chaos, shouts, screams, and grunts of pain echo behind me as I flip around. Middle was glaring at me with such fire, it could burn me if it was real.

I snarl, taking a protective stance. Anna was trying to separate the boys from fighting as I held my eyes with the man.

"WEE UO WEE UO WE UO!!!" Sounded the police sirens.

In less than a minute the place was surrounded. I backed against the wall, picking up the shocked boy as Anna transformed back into human; a naked human.

I quickly cover the boy's eyes, though his shock kept him frozen, "Damn Anna! We need to get you some clothes!"

She rolls her eyes as we crept past the line of police cars, almost invisible.

"Turn here!" Anna whispers in my ear as we rush down the street, people slowly coming out to see what the fuss is about. I slam the door open with my foot, setting down the shaking boy.

Anna chuckled slightly, going to the closest clothing rack and picking out a bra and underwear, "Welcome to the dress store!"

~~~~~~
~~~~~~

Hey guys. I'm really sorry for my lack of being on on wattpad and not sticking to my due dates. But now I'm back now that family business calmed down slightly. I want to thank you guys who are still reading. This story took a weird turn and for that I apologies.

~

Anyway, I hope you guys like and if you can please check out my recent story: Once Connected

Once Connected is another Mythical Story that has a kinda of some flow as this one. Please just check it out? It would mean a lot. Thanks <3

Chapter 25- Too Slow

Athena and Linda chatter excitedly with their beautiful dresses in hand. Anna was still shopping around for accessories while I didn't even have a dress. I sigh as my hand skim over, again, all of the beautiful dresses. None of them were, me. And all could see that.

The little man mumbles to himself as he runs up to me with tape measures, pins, and all sorts of other things falling out of his pocket. His name was Mr.Grim, he was our dressmaker. Besides the name, he was a very friendly person.

I sigh again as I step onto the platform, half-naked and he begins taking measurements of my body. He mumbles as his eyes twinkle in concentration, "I will send the dress to you as soon as possible." He said with his gruff voice.

I nod my head, mumbling a thank you as I looked over where Mat and the boys were tossing a football around. Mat was the boy I saved from the gang. He was a magic weirder and he was only ten years old. "That boy..... He was very powerful magic stored in him...."I nod my head, smiling slightly, "Then it becomes my job to project him.... My brother grew up without me. It's time for someone who needs me to receive me."

Mr.Grim gives a nod as he finishes taking the measurements of my body and I slip off the platform. Anna flashes a bright smile at me, all her clothing and accessories in her hand, "Got the measurements done?"I nod my head as I slip into a pair of jeans and t-shirt, "Mhmm."

"Come on ladies! Can't shop all day! The boys finished two hours ago!" Athena jokes.I throw a smirk as I exit the shop and take all the clothing from the girls, "it's not our fault the boys are that sloppy with cloth shopping."

"Excuse me madam, I could help but over-heard that you think boys are sloppy?" A smooth voice asks behind me. I keep walking straight, not looking behind me though a smile crept onto my lips, "Of course, why do you think we girls always get what we want? We use boys' sloppiness for our own uses." I stop at Léo's other car, unlocking it and placing everyone's clothes in."Tsk, tsk, tsk. Such a tease you are...." The voice behind me says as two warm and sturdy arms wrap around my waist, pulling me into the body behind me. I yelped I am gentle crushed into a firm chest. Ethan snuggles his face into my neck, sighing happily.

I purse my lips as I just stood there, with Ethan clutching me possessively. "Hey playboy, get off of me!" I feel him smile against my neck as he takes a deep inhale, "now why would I want to do that runner? So you can run off again?"

I lean against Ethan. "Most likely, it's fun when I play hard-to-get," I smirk.Ethan takes another deep breath before his fingers crawl up my sides and onto my ribs, "if you will be a bad girl I will have to punish you...." "You wouldn't dare," I whisper dangerously."Try me," he whispers back before he starts to tickle me. I explode with laughter, squirming to get away. "Make it stop, I'll listen! I'll listen!" I yell through giggles. He stops, flashing his famous smirk. Then I duck, quickly slipping out of his arms and dashing towards Athena. I grab her hand and pull her away from Jack. She yelps before joining me in my run with both of us laughing. We freeze behind a car as Jack and Ethan's faces both had this annoyed look to them.

"Told you blood-sucker, when someone is sexy, they gotta play hard to get," I wink. Ethan's face softens before determination takes his face and his smirk reappears, "Oh. So that's what it's going to take?"Jack laughs, "Bro, you wouldn't be able to do that for the life of you. Sorry, bro, to take down a sexy beast, you need to be a sexy beast. Like me!" Jack dramatically does a hair flip causing Athena and I to explode with laughter.

"You wish you were sexy Jack!" Laughs Anna as she runs to the car, which me and Athena were behind, with Linda. Léo and Will join the other two boys with smirks and annoyed looks playing on their features.

I jump up onto the roof of the car, "Where's Mat?""In the car playing my phone," replies Jack, winking at Athena. I see her blush a bit before throwing an air kiss at him. He turns red. I give a little nod of my head, "Alright. Let the games begin!" I shout to the people in the empty parking lot.Instantly Ethan charges at me but with an easy jump, I flip over him and burst into a run. Soon shouts and laughter take over the parking lot as the boys tried to catch us girls and us girls trying to free each other from the boys.

"Gotcha!" A voice yells as their arms wrap around my waist. I smirk, "Wrong one Jack!" I kick him gently on this thigh causing him to drop me. Then I dash, laughing as he rolls his eyes playfully.

"Thud!" Athena and I crash into each other, falling onto the floor. We burst into laughter as we try to catch our breaths on the dirty asphalt. My cheeks throbbed from the amount of laughter. I take a deep breath and quickly look around. Léo was holding Anna tight, resting his head on her head as she looked relaxed in his arms. Will and Linda were kissing. I yelp as I am picked up bridal style from the floor.

"Ethan!" I yell as at the same time I hear Athena laughing, "Jack!"I snap my head towards them as Jack finally makes the move. He finally kisses her. Her eyes flickered in surprise before she closed them and kissed Jack back.Yes! I do a silent cheer as Ethan's voice snaps my attention back to him, "My turn."

A surprised moan escapes my lips as his soft lips over take mine. It was a quick peck, but it still left me dazed.I shake my head, trying to get myself out of the daze as Ethan smirks, "Did I catch you, my little hard-to-get?"

I sigh defeated, "Yes, my blood-sucking dragon. Now put me down!"Ethan chuckles as he places me back down onto the ground.

This next week should be fun.

Chapter 26- War Among Lovers

"Clink!" Go the keys as I throw them into the granite counter. I sigh slightly as I collapse onto the couches, rubbing my forehead, "Stupid teachers....."

A door opens and I hear a person enter the room. Jack collapses onto a opposite couch, grinning, "What's up little duck?"

"What?" I ask, annoyed.

Jack shrugs, "What's up?"

I moan, throwing my head back against the couch and shutting my eyes, "I sent Mat to fourth grade in Mythical Academy, but freaking teachers saw me and started yelling at how such a bad student I was and I would never be accepted! Ugh!"

Jack purses his lips, "What are you doing bad in?"

"Math...."

"Omg, I suck at math too!" Anna pipes up as she jumps onto the third couch. Athena mumbles something about school as she grabs an apple from the kitchen and collapses next to Anna.

Linda and Will take the seats next to Jack as a deep voice smirks, "You know, I'm pretty good at math...."

I groan louder causing chuckles to erupt through the crowd as Ethan leans over me. His electrifying blue eyes holding mine as he flashes that famous smirk, "I could tutor you."

I raise my eyebrows with my head still back, "Oh really? How are you going to do that blood-sucker?"

"Easy. All you have to do is add the bed. I'll subtract the clothes, you divide the legs, and I'll multiply." Ethan wiggles his eyebrows.

My jaw drops. "Nope nope nope!" I rapidly stand up, walking away from that bastard of a vampire dragon thing, "In your dreams lover boy!" I say, crossing my arms.

Ethan winks at me, "mmm, yes, in my dreams that does come true."

"Ew! Ew! Okay okay, you know what, I'm done! I'm done!" I throw my hands up quickly walking out of the house. "God damn vampire dragon thingy..." I mumble to myself as I storm to the chilly outside.

It was pitch back. The stars shining brightly and the moon giving its blue glow. There were no lights, only the deep blue sky and the blackness of the forest.

"Ready for the 'real night'?" Ethan asks from behind me. I nod my head I lean into him, smirking at how he tensed.

Aw poor baby, not used to me being comfortable with him.

"Yes. You promised me a while ago a 'real night'."

His arms wrap around me, as he nuzzles his head into my neck, "I know, I just wasn't sure you were ready especially when you hid your power...."

I sigh as I hear the couples from inside start to move around.

Turns out, K-8th grade, or primary school, in Mythical Academy is at night time. So we don't have to worry about Mat and have the night to ourselves.

"So my lover birds, ready to go?" Athena chuckles. I instantly lift off Ethan before smirking, "I can say the same to you, lover bird."

Athena blushes, shuffling a little away from Jack and closer to me as everyone else leaves the house. Ethan steps up, placing a possessive hold on my shoulders.

My friends smirk and begin to make kissy faces at me and Ethan as his back was turned. Like a toddler my tongue darts out before I cross my arms and annoyingly look straight.

"Alright everyone! As everyone knows, tonight is 'real night'. We had a load of games and activities for the whole night..... But first rules."

Everyone gives a little groan before Ethan shoots them a shushing look. He clears his throat and continues, "No sexual contact or activities please, and otherwise, have fun!"

Ethan winks at me causing my cheeks to turn scarlet. "Now for the team s......"

My eyes widen as I get an idea. I break away from Ethan's clutch, stepping up, before shouting, "Boys vs Girls!"

I freeze. Why the heck did I just want to be in control all of a sudden? I chuckle uncertainly before looking back to Ethan. He was actually thinking about the idea.

Everyone was.

What? Why are they accepting me? This is weird....

Athena, Anna, and Linda begin to chant, "Boys vs Girls. Boys vs Girls. Boy vs Girls!"

Soon the boys join in and everyone is but Ethan are chanting, "Boys vs Girls!"

I turn around smirking at Ethan with the chanters behind me, "Do we have a deal, team captain?" I stick out my hand, stupidly grinning.

Ethan raises an eyebrow before smirking, "Deal....."

He grabs my hand and we shake. Though shivers were running up and down my spine from his touch.

I grin, "Let the games begin!" Again.

Chapter 27- The Capture

"Click clack!" Goes my nerf gun as us girls prepare for war. All of us were in dark camo outfits that where tight, flexible, and full of pockets. We were locked and loaded. Our pockets were filled with knives, nerf bullets and guns, gas bombs, and all sorts of other trinkets. Our outfits, luckily, don't get shredded when we transformed, so we also have that up our sleeves.

"Alright ladies, we ready to take the boys down?" I ask, my loaded gun on leaning against my hip as I place the bow over my head and onto my shoulders.

Linda, Athena, and Anna all grinned. All of them had the same outfits with high pony tails and all were full of toy weapons. I press play on the phone. The sounds of giggles and gossip took over the room as I shut off the lights and only turned on the bathroom light.

We overheard a little birdy telling us that the boys think we are having a make-up party to amaze the boys with our looks. Ha! How surprised they are going to be!

I give the hand signal and the girls and I go to our hiding places around the small room. The boys' territory is the deep forest and the girls' territory was the house. The equal territory was the forest area between the two territories, or the forest around the house.

I sense the boys coming through my mate bond and I grin. I lock my gun into place and catch eyes with all my girlfriends."It's time!" I mouth out.

The door creeps open and the first dark covered person walks in. The another, then another, and finally the last one.

Their hushed whispers were loud and clear in the silence of the room. My eyes catch the ones of my teammates. With a quick nod, we silently scurry around the furniture, getting closer to the figures. My head turned sideways as my dragon vision caused the room to glow green with night vision.

The three figures were sulking near the bathroom door where the light was on the the giggling from the phone was heard. But, they don't know it's coming from the phone...

A firm but warm hand suddenly snaps around my mouth, hiding my squeal of surprise."Sshhh little runner," a deep husky voice whispers in my ear as their other arm is now wrapped around my body tightly, "Don't want to give away to your team that I'm not at the door, now do we?"

A low growl rumbles from my throat as Ethan gives a low chuckle, still holding me prisoner in the darkness of the room.My finger tips crawl toward my belt though my arms were still tightly held in place.

My eyes widen as I see the three dark figures multiple into six. Freak! They brought manikins! Ethan whispers huskily in my ear as the boys start to sneak around, crawling to the girls, "your team mates won't even see them coming, since you are not there to warn then.

My hands grasp tightly the smoke bomb as I give a growl. "Now you get to watch your team be abducted, love.""Ow!" Shouts Ethan as I bite him, making his grasp release on me.

"Girls look out!" I scream as I unpin the bomb, throwing it on the ground. Instantly the room fills with the white smoke. The girls all had their masks on and were silently creeping out as the boys were in a coughing fit on the floor. The smoke isn't toxic or anything, the just blinds the enemy for a second and it will blind you too if you do not have the proper mask.

I jump out of Ethan's arms and run for the door. Made it! My feet take me into the forest, the neutral territory as I meet up with the rest of my gals."What happened?" Asks Athena, panting for we leaned against the tree. "Eth--.... Ethan..... Wasn't part of the group of shadows we saw come in...." I wheeze. "They came in then places manikins to trick you guys. Ethan held me tight so I could scream...."

Anna smirks before wiggling her eyebrows, "You mean so you couldn't moan?"My jaw drops, "Ew no! He said no sexual contact!"

"He is a bad boy and rule breaker...." Athena chuckles.I give her playfully glare before we burst into laughter. "Alright ladies!" Anna says happily to bring our attention back, "how are we going to get the boys back?"

But before any of us can usher a word, hoodied-men jump from the bushes and quickly cover our mouths with duck and quickly take us down.

"Come on, little dragon, time to see your daddy."

Chapter 28- Love or Life

I scream as the duck tap is ripped off my mouth. I was in a dungeon room with my girlfriends and I all on our knees and tied up. Black-hoodies men surrounded us like body guards, keeping a tight circle. The room itself was made up of stone, there were no windows. The room was illuminated by old-fashioned torches on the walls. In front of us was a large plush red throne. And who was standing at that throne? Sheila, of course.

She glares down upon me, though keeps her tense posture near the throne. A familiar voice echoes out, "Your highness! I have retrieved the girls......"

My head flips around as I snarl, "You bastard! Why did you do this!" I struggle against my ropes as I try to attack Pierce. "Because I paid him too, honey." A deep voice echoed.

A growl rumbled in my throat as my head snaps back to the King, or my father. He was dressed in golden king robes and was slowly walking towards his throne."I'm not your honey! But I see you finally got that kingdom you wanted, Daniel."I hiss. My hate-filled eyes were locked onto my 'father'. The girls had the same hateful glares.

"Yes you are my little dragon. I am your father, and since I am king, that makes you a princess. If you stop fighting I can give you all the riches of the world. I just need a few experiments to be done with you.""Why the fuck would I want to be Princess? I don't want all the God damn riches of the world, I want to see my MATE and all my FRIENDS safe at the pack house, with you gone or dead!"Daniel, or my father, purses his lips, "I'm afraid I cannot do that. However, if you do not cooperate, I will have to send you down to the torture chamber, my dear. And your friends too." "I will never team with you!" I spit.

Daniel flicks his hand as Sheila gets a strange spark in her eyes, "Guards take them down to the chamber."

Then all of us girls began screaming and shouting and fighting with all of our strength. But it was no use. We were thrown into the chamber like we were feathers. I send one hateful glare around the room, catching Pierce's guilty eyes. I mouth out, "You. Will. Pay." Then the door slams behind us and we were pushed in through the dark dungeon. We topple into a cold stone room and the bars shut and lock with a loud, "CLANG!"

I grasp the metal bars that held us. What have I gotten my friends into?I turn to my friends and look at them with sorrowful eyes, "I'm so sorry girls for dragging you into this. I promise when we get home I will leave the pack and reduce your worries."Their mouths drop, "KATE! WHAT ARE YOU THINKING?!! We don't want you to leave! We all bring problems into the pack, but we all share a bond of love that none of us can break." Athena, Anna, and Linda all flash these dazzling smiles."Oh girls, I love you guys so much!" I broke into tears and rushed at them, grabbing them into a hug.When this is over, I am defiantly choosing to stay with them.

--------2 days later----------

Daniel mumbles something to his scientist while I was shivering in pain on the floor.The last two days of torture was unbearable. Everything from spikes, to rocks, to boiling water, to fire was used on me. I was curled up in a ball, tears gently running down my face as I was dreaming for escape, and my body slowly shutting down.

"Crash!" An object sounded in the dungeon. My eyes shut as the pain swept me away into a safer place, a carefree place. A place were I would no longer have to live to go to. I whisper in my head, "take me away....."

Warm hands grabbed me and I feel a faint buzz of energy from a mate bond. "Kate! Kate! Kate! No, no, no! You can't die on me!" A pained voice shrills next to me, though their voice sounded miles away. "We got to get out of here! The place is gonna blow!" another familiar voice yells. I feel my limp body being lifted as something warm drips onto my lip and into my mouth. I see the tunnel of light and I begin to float closer. But then, something stops me.

"Kate. Swallow this. Please. Please stay alive, I can't loose you! I-I love you......." The voice whimpers as I feel myself being lifted and carried away. I freeze in my way toward the light before slowly feeling myself return to my body. I gulp down the warm liquid before my consciousness shuts down and I am carried into a darkness that might mean my death.

Chapter 29- Love Wins

"Beep. Beep. Beep."I numbly open my eyes. Everything was blurry and hush whispering was heard from the side.I blink a few times, and slowly a hospital room comes into view."Beep. Beep. Beep." I look around, I was connected to a heart rate monitor. Tubes and other wires were connected to me and I blink again.

I shuffle in my bed before doubling over into a coughing fit.

"Kate!" A familiar voice shouts with worry. A warmth fills me as I suck in a breath. I lean my head back against the pillow and give a small smile to Ethan. "Hey there blood-sucker." I weakly whisper and give a small smile.

"Hey." He smiles, tears welling up in his eyes as he takes my hand. "Oh Kate, I thought you were never going to wake up."He squeezes his eyes shut and looks down, squeezing my hand like his life depended on it.

I sit up, slowly regaining my energy."E-Ethan, w-where am I?" I look around in fear, noticing this wasn't the pack house, or the mythical hospital.Ethan sighs, "You are in a human hospital."

"What?! Why?" I instantly tense and look up at Ethan with fearful eyes. A shining light flashes into my eye and I wince slightly. I look at the fingers holding my hand and gasp. "You're engaged?!?"

Tears fill in my eyes, "W-who-W-Why--what?"Ethan sighs, "you have been in coma for the last month and a half. My father, the vampire King, kicked you out and sent you here for you couldn't agree if you wanted to stay with us.... He then made me get engaged with Sheila; not knowing what her father and she did to us. But I couldn't get him to listen." Ethan gives a hurt scoff, "Anna, Léo, Will, and Linda left the pack. Athena and Jack finally got together, and when they did, they also left... Mat, the boy you saved from the alleyway was given to a foster home. They love him like their own son. Though they do not have any children other than Mat. Still, the pack broke apart and Daniel is still ruling an underground kingdom with Pierce at his side."

My heart breaks. Everything collapsed. I again was a free runner. However, my friends were free runners too.....

I could see his eyes get watery. I gently caress his face. He was still my mate. I wanted him to be happy with his life, even if my sister took it from him. "I'm sorry...."Ethan leans against my hand, his eyes closing and he sighs in partial relief. When is gorgeous blue eyes snap open again, they were full of confidence. "No Kate. I am sorry, I am your mate. I should have cancelled the wedding, I should have never given up on you, I should have....." He pauses and catches my eyes. "It's not that I should have. I will do.... I'll be right back Kate. I have some calls to make."

He releases my hand and starts to exit the hospital room. Instantly my loneliness gets to me. I didn't want him to leave!

"Wait Ethan!" I call after him. However, he already left my room and was strutting toward the hospital exit. I find hidden energy in my limbs as my scar bursts into life. I rip out the tubes and shuffle off my bed. I roll off and land with a hard 'thud' on the floor. I groan out in pain but then my animal side gives me more power. I wobble up onto my two feet and shuffle towards the cabinet in my room. Surprisingly, I find my clothes there. I quickly get changed, my muscles slowly coming to life as my animal side and scar gave me power to do so.

Then, I run. Shouts of surprise are thrown my way as the humans who took care of me just saw their coma patient running way. I had to get to Ethan! I could see his fading figure as I get closer to the door.

"SLAM!" I get knocked to the ground. I look up in fear as I see a guard holding me down.I see Ethan get into his car and the car drive off.

"No!" I shout and start to wiggle. I throw the cop off of me and yell back, "SORRY!" Then I run outside but Ethan's car was already speeding away down the street.

"Ethan!" I scream, but with no avail. Stomping my foot in anger, I look around. The hospital was in the middle of a forest. Hearing human footsteps running toward me, I dart sideways and run towards the forest. My animal power roars inside me as I jump into super speed. I run and run and run deeper and deeper into the forest. Finally, the sound of human footsteps disappears from my extra-sensitive hearing.

I close my eyes and concentrate. My bones start popping and scraping as I feel them start changing and moving. My body elongates, and my skin turns silver. A wind whistles through and I shut my eyes as my transformation finishes. Opening my eyes, I grin, flashing my fangs. I was back into dragon form.

I jump into the air, and fall back down. I have never actually lifted-off before. I try again, and suddenly, I was high in the air as wind catches my wings and lifts me upward. I was flying!I mentally grin and push my wings down, shooting myself forward. The trees fly by like lightning as I zoom through the skies, following Ethan's car. As I get closer, I notice the top open. I fly a little ahead, and swoop down lower. Then I transformed back. Just as I had calculated, I perfectly fell down and landed right through the open roof in the co-drivers seat.

"Woah! What the f*ck Kate!" Shouts Ethan in fear before calming down. "Kate! What the f*ck are you thinking!?!" He shouts in worry.

I shrug, trying to cover my naked body the best I could with my arms, "I had to tell you something."

Ethan grits his teeth, "What did you have to tell me that was so important that you had to transform midair to land in my car?!?"

"I love you too." I whisper.

"What?" Ethan's tone drops. "You told me you loved me. I love you too." I whisper back.

Ethan glances sideways at me, seeing if I was telling the truth. But I wasn't lying, I was dead serious.

"Oh f*ck Kate. I love you too!" He lunged at me enveloping my lips with his. I freeze in surprise before closing my eyes and giving in. His soft lips moved against mine and I moan in bliss. His hand goes into my hair and the other around my back, pushing me against him. He gently nibbles at my bottom lip, wanting entrance. I give in.Finally, I break the kiss in fear and the need for breath. "Who is driving the car?!?" Ethan's face pales, "Nobody is." His head snaps toward the road and he screams, "We are going to crash!"

I scream and squeeze my eyes shut. But when only the peaceful rumbling on the engine is heard I open my eyes to find Ethan smirking with his hand barely touching the wheel.

"It's a self-driving car if it needs to be." He says simply.I glare at him, "You bastard of a blood-sucker."He smirks and looks at me. "You know you love me.""I do no--!" He cuts me off with kiss. He breaks it and looks back at the road. I lick my tingling lips, "I do love you."

He smirks with victory. "So where we going anyway?" I ask.

"Not we, me." Ethan's jaw clenches. I roll my eyes, "Ya, as if I would let that happen. You can't worry for my safety, for if you lock me up, I will only escape and put myself in more danger." I grin.

Ethan glances at me sideways. He then chuckles, "I can't persuade you otherwise?""Nope!" I grin, popping the 'p'.

He smiles, "Fine. We are going to the palace, to talk to my father."My animal side purrs at how he uses 'we'.

I scrunch my eyebrows, "to talk about what?""What Daniel did to you, my pack, and everything else."My eyes glance down at his ring, "What about the wedding?"

He looks down at his ring and snarls, "F*ck the wedding!" He rips off the ring and throws it out the window.

I can't help but grin. I tilt my head, "No cussing vampire..."He chuckles. "God damn I missed you.""I missed you too. Can I have some clothes?"Ethan glances down at me and I blush.

He sighs and points to the back seat. "Some of your clothes are in the white bag over there."

I narrow my eyes, "Why do you have clothes?"He shuffles, embarrassedly, "Um, they had your scent and were the last thing I had of you left." His voice breaks as my features soften.I kiss him gently on the cheek, "Well,

I'm here now."I crawl to the back and quickly put on some clothes. I crawl back to the front."Oh and by the way, I missed you too." I say.

Chapter 30- Back Together, Fighting Together

E than pulls up at a little gas station and pancake house by the road. I look around and furrow my eyebrows, "Why are we here?" I ask.

Ethan sighs, "You'll see." He gets out of the car and I follow. The gas station was little looking and the pancake house seemed like a quiet little family owned business. Everything around here was forest, so pine trees were growing around the two little buildings. Ethan takes my hand as we walk toward the pancake house. I look up at him and smile, tingles running up my arm.

We walk in sync toward the house and enter together. The restaurant was fairly busy. It had white walls and dark wood booths. A very 'home' design.

My mouth drops and tears well-up in my eyes as I scan the restaurant, "Anna! Linda! Athena!" I yell in joy. Their heads pop up as they hear their names. "Kate!" They yell together and jump out of their seats and run towards me. I meet them half-way and hug them. We sign in happiness. As I break the group hug, I wipe away a tear, "I missed you guys so much!" All of them were crying too, "We missed you too Kate! We tried to visit you at the hospital but because we left the pack, the vampire King would not let us in..." Anna explained."since the hospital was in pack territory..." Athena quickly added. I sob again and smile at the same time.

Ethan comes up behind me."Ethan...." The girls say with pain. The other boys quickly get up from the table and come to protect their girls. That is, after they hugged me and I cried some more.

Ethan looks down and stammers, "I'm sorry I left you guys....I'm sorry I listened to my father....I'm...."I stop Ethan. He looks down at me as I face my friends, my pack mates, my family. "He is sorry. He won't be marrying Sheila, for his hand belongs to me."

My old pack smirks as surprise takes Ethan's face. "He is also right now going to talk with the vampire King." I finish. "Would you like to join us and get the pack back together?!"

"Oh hell yes!" Shouts Athena, catching the attention of some diners. "Look, we might have hated your decision, Ethan, but we are always part of your pack."

Jack adds, "That's the one thing our parents did right-- to bring us all together."

I grin, "Well then, what are we waiting for?"The girls all clap their hands together and run back over to their table to get their stuff,

As we waited, Ethan's hands wrap around my waist. He nuzzles his face in my hair, and kisses my neck. "You know I love you?"

I smile, "Yes. Do you know I hate you?"

I fell him grin against my neck. I lean against him, and sigh, "I love you too."

Ethan sighs, "I still have to claim you, you know."I tense, before sighing also, "You have my permission."Now Ethan tenses, "what?""I love you blood-sucker and I want you to be mine and me to be yours."Ethan hugs me tighter, "I love you more than you can even imagine."

Before I knew it, Ethan had connected all of his pack back together and even made me part of the pack. Let's just say the process was unpleasant.

Now we were all in four separate cars, each couple in their own car; driving towards the kingdom of vampires.

The forest slowly became the city, the city slowly became mountains, and the mountains slowly became the ocean. We kept driving and driving until a stone castle was seen. My jaw drops, "Your dad lives in an actual castle?!?"

Ethan's grip on the wheel tighten, "Yes." He says coldly.

I'm sensing some family issues.

We pull up to the gates and are allowed in. The castle literally looked like a old-fashion 17th century castle.We park in front of the castle doors and hop out. Vampire servants super-speed to our side and take our keys to park our cars elsewhere. A vampire butler leads us inside of the castle.

Ethan looks around coldly and wraps his hand around my waist tightly. The butler leads us through the huge castle through golden room to golden room. We finally end up in a high ceiling hallway with paintings from the olden times hanging on the walls. At the end of the hallway were huge, 16 foot doors with gold engraved on them. The Butler that brought us here bows and quickly says, "The King will see you shortly," Before bowing again and scurrying off.

The group stands around, everyone tense. Finally, the doors creak open. A deep voice booms, "Come in!" Everyone shuffles in with hateful glares on their faces.

The throne room was humongous! A red carpet lead to the throne that was places higher than anything else in the room. Behind the throne were windows that took up the whole wall, giving a view of the mountains and ocean. Everything else around the room was elegantly designed with expensive furniture, decorations, and paintings. "Come forward!" The voice from the throne booms.

We walks up towards the throne and stop at the edge. Then we bow. The king steps up from his throne walks up to us.

"You may stand!" His voice leaked with power. We stand and Ethan's grip on me tightens. I finally get a good look at the king.He looked like he was in his late twenties! The vampire King was pale white with Ethan's blue eyes, but blonde hair. He looked slippery(metaphorically speaking), and like a trickster. He was frowning, and his gold suit and cape showed he was rich.I did not like him already.

Ethan held his head up high, "Father, we need to talk about the deal and the wedding." The king's eyes flicker to Ethan's hand, which was wrapped around my waist.

"What did you do?" The king's voice got dangerously low and his eyes turned red. I gulped.

"I found my mate, and decided I will marry her. Instead of her evil brat sister and I threw away the ring."The king hissed and pointed to me, not taking his eyes of his son. "I want this girl, your mate, OUT!" Ethan's grip tightened even more on me.I gaze with hate at the king. "Yes, your highness." I reply for Ethan. He looks down at me with worry as I step away from his grasp and come right up to the king. The king was shocked.

I hold his red eyes with furry, "If you hurt Ethan in any single way, I will kill you."I turn around without a second of thought and exit the room.The heavy doors shut behind me and instantly yelling was heard. I squeeze my eyes shut, praying for my mate to be okay. My eyes get watery.

"Are you alright deary?" A soft woman's voice asks. My head snaps toward the sound and I quickly wipe the tears. "Yes, I am just worried for my mate."

The woman dark green eyes fill with understanding. She walks over to me. Her silk maroon gown hugging her perfect curves perfectly and contrasting against her pitch black hair also perfectly. She also looked like she was in her late twenties. Though her eyes showed the wisdom of age.

"Who is your mate dear?" She asks gently, her hand touching my shoulder. I felt relaxed with this woman. She was powerful, but she didn't abuse it."Prince Ethan." I say quietly. The woman's eyes widen before a smile grows. "Your mate is my son?" I blink and look up to her.

"Oh my gosh, your highness! I'm so sorry! Please forgive me!" I quickly bow down. Now this woman, has earned the honor to be called her highness.

The queen laughs, "Please dearie! Call me Marie."I nod my head, standing up, "Yes Marie."

"Now tell me. Why are you crying for Ethan?"

"Well...." I start. Then the journey from the moment I met Ethan to right now was told.

Chapter 31- Love and War

The queen was furious. "My husband did WHAT?""He made Ethan marry Sheila after Daniel tortured us and I was sent into a normal hospital because of my coma." I repeat.

The queen shakes her head, gritting my teeth. "We need to talk with my husband right now."

I nod my head, I like her so much!"Can you break down the door sweetie?" She asks. "Of course Marie!" I say with a smile as my body begins to transform.As the transformation finishes, the queen stares at me and my shimmer scales with awe. Before cursing to herself, "My husband is stupid!" She mentions to the door. I grin and rear up on my hind legs and slam into the door. The door creaks and groans. "BOOM!!!!" Echoes the castle as the doors drops. The king's mouth drops open.

"Charles!!!" Yells the queen, strutting toward the throne room. The king visibly pales. "Y-yes my darling?"

"How dare you force our baby boy into a marriage that is not right for him! How dare you make him go into a marriage that isn't with his mate! Look, I know we are not mates and you want to follow in your father's footsteps by making him marry a woman that you think fits best for him, but that is not right!"

"H-honey..."

Queen Marie holds up her hand for him to stay quiet. He listens and I grin.Marie sighs, "I've learned to love you Charles, but our son has found his mate." She places her hand on my scales and I shiver, transforming back. King Charles' mouth drops even more. Ethan smirks proudly.

"Don't you think our kingdom should fall to a ruler who has his other half to rule with him? To always have his side? To make him more powerful than before? Or would you rather have a weak ruler who always is gone drinking away because he hates his wife who is spending all of his money?" She scolds him.

The king mumbles and looks down, "The strong ruler."

The queen continues, "Exactly! Did you even listen what Daniel Howl did to our son's first and only pack? A pack that is the strongest pack currently?!? No! Of course not!" Queen Marie sighs, "Charles, I really do love you. But don't take away our son's opportunity for true love."

The girls and I share a look and grin. Girl power!!!

King Charles sighs and walks over to his queen. "Marie, I love you too. And I will cancel the wedding." He kisses her before walking over to me. "So um...."

"Kate..." I finish for him."Um, yes. Kate. May I ask what your animal is?"I smile, "Of course your highness. I am an animal transformer that is lunar eclipse dragon with certain elemental powers like ice and electricity."

The king nods, "Kate, would you like to join this family and become the Luna of our son's pack through marriage."

I grin, "I would absolutely love too. But...."The king tenses."Only Ethan can ask me to marry him,"

The queen and Ethan smirk.Ethan walks over to me and gets down on one knee.I blink. I didn't expect him to already have ring!!!"Kate.... Will you marry me? I know this isn't quite the romantic place but-""Yes!" I squeal and kiss Ethan on the lips. He smiles as I break the kiss and hold out my hand.

Gently, he puts the ring on my finger. It was a silver dragon ring. The face connected with the tail to create a ring. The eye was a sapphire blue gem. I was crying from happiness.

"Ethan, let me see the other ring." I say.Ethan blinks in surprise but pulls out another dragon ring, exact to mine, except with a red gem for the eye.I take his hand and hold his eyes, "Prince Ethan, I would love to accept your hand in marriage." I slip the ring on his finger and he grins. He sweeps me off my feet and kisses me.

My girlfriends go into applause before being also swept off their feet by their mates.

"Do you know I love you?" He asks with his eyes shinning with awe. "And that I would never have been able to do this without you?"

I grin, "Do you know I love you? And that this would also have not been done without you?"

Ethan smirks, "Absolutely." I smile and he kisses me again.

The sound of trumpets sounds in the distance and everyone freezes. The king, however, visibly tenses.A light laugh sounds through the large throne room. Ethan possessively clutches me as his narrowed eyes search the room. "Pierce." He hisses.

The air shimmers ahead of us and Pierce magically appears. He smirks, "Hello family...."Ethan growls as Pierce scans all of us. His eyes lock with mine before glancing down to my hand. He raises an eyebrow, "What's this brother?" He points to the ring on my finger.

"She is MINE!" Ethan hisses. Pierce's blue eyes flash red. Jack and Athena tense, Léo and Ana growl, while Will clutches Linda tighter. "Don't you dare hurt her." Anna snarls as they slowly gather around me. I couldn't feel prouder to be part of this pack.

Pierce looks toward King Charles. "Dad, you let them come back together? And you let the marriage CANCEL?!?"

King Charles holds his head up high, "Yes."Pierce ponders the thought. His eyes move across my pack, to his parents and back. He smirks, "Then the war has begun."

Chapter 32- The Demon King

Pierce disappears as soon as he announced the war. Trumpets sound again and all of us rush to the window. There, on the mountain stood an army. Dark Shadows shrieked and screamed with laughter and were flying around like pesky flies. Jack gasps, "Shadow demons....." The demons flew forward, leading the army as it grew bigger and bigger. Hundreds of rogues lined up with weapons at hand. Each of them with red unnatural eyes, and were working together a little too........ Perfectly.

"Possessys....." Anna whispered, watching the red eye mythicals. Athena bit her lip and I glance sideways at her.

"A possessy hurt you, didn't they?" I ask with a gentle tone. Athena nods, her eyes fogging up. Jack notices her change in mood and places a hand on her shoulder. She looks him in the eye and I see this powerful emotion go through both of them. Athena's expression became hard as she turned back to look at the approaching army.

King Charles sighs, "Come, we must meet the Demon King and find out his terms for surrender." He pauses and look over to Marie, "Dearie?"

At this point Queen Marie's mood was hardened also. She nods her head silently and shuts her eyes.In a few seconds all of us were teleported right in front of the army. I look at Marie in surprise. She gives me a small smile, "One of my powers..."I nod in understanding. The army stares at us before parting like flies, completely in sync. Everyone had armor, and spears at hand but did not give us a second glance, like they didn't care about the war, or themselves for that matter.

A huge black beast of a horse trots forward. The rider was another beast in itself. The rider's armor was pitch black and the area where his eyes should be were two piercing pupils that were the color of blood. Black smoke billowed from behind him like a cloak and a black, whispy crown sat on his head.

Linda gulped in fear, "The demon king...."I growled.

The Demon King kept looking down at us, un-effected by our glares. After a few more seconds, a white stallion comes riding down next to him. Who was the rider of this horse? Sheila.

"Hi baby-boo." Sheila said with a seductive tone, flutter her eye lashes at Ethan. He grits his teeth, looking like he was ready to kill her. I put my hand on his shoulder. My scar began burning up. My eyes hold his. He had to remain stable, for all of us.

Sheila looks at my hand and hate fills her eyes. Her dreadful gaze switches to Ethan. "Baby, don't tell me you sided with this b*tch?!" Everyone just watched in silence. The army, was looking away, like robots, the demon king was watching with interest but his emotions were hidden by the mask, and my pack was watching, ready to attack.

"I never sided with you Sheila!" Spits Ethan, "I always belonged to your sister!" I couldn't help but feel something flutter with happiness in my heart. Yet my brain looked at this in horror. He did not just say that....

Sheila's face turns red with hatred. "You bastard.... Daddy, can you take out the trash? I don't even want to try to save my mate!"

She turns away like a spoiled brat except my expression remained one of horror. Daddy.... The Demon King..... The Torture..... Pierce..... The experiments.....

I hold the demon king's empty red eyes, "Daniel Howl...."A deep robotic laugh sounds through, coming from the armor. "Hello sweetie.... Have you missed me?"

My packs' mouths dropped. My angry took over my fear, "You? You are the demon king?!" I shout."Why yes, my dragon. I am, but I am not here to stand here while you let your anger out on me. I am here for the details of your surrender, if you accept that is."

I cross my arms, "Well?"My pack stood around me protectively, though the vampire king and queen were completely shocked that the person they wanted their son to marry was the demon king's spoiled daughter.

"I want to rule the mythical world. Sheila will marry Ethan, and the rest will be banished from the land. Though Kate shall stay and be the dragon of the kingdom." The deep robot voice of Daniel sounds. "If you win, I shall leave."

I snort at the thought.Daniel continues, "And I will never touch you again.""Liar!" Athena screams.

Daniel's furious eyes snap to her, "When you do surrender, I'm cutting off your tongue little goddess!"Athena shuts her mouth though Jack takes a threading step toward Daniel.

Little quiet Linda snaps first. Though all were hating Daniel, Linda was blood-boiling mad, "We will never surrender to you son of a b*tch! We are family and we will never give up these lands to you, or any of your minions!

Our family will never be separated or forced into something they don't want! So why don't you get the f*ck away!!! We are accepting the war!"

Ethan and I both looked toward Linda in surprise, she was always so shy and scared. Then again, Daniel was the demon king. I smugly look back toward the also shocked Daniel. He regains himself and smirks from behind the mask,"Fine. The war has begun."

With that Daniel pulls a pitch black sword from his belt and points it at us. All of the army's eyes snap toward us, simultaneously. My horror returns, he was controlling ALL of them. In sync they all grin sadistic smiles as their spears are tilted toward us. My fear began to rise as I pale. This wasn't fair! He wasn't playing fairly!

"He is a demon! He doesn't know how to play fairly!" King Charles yells, reading my thoughts, "Marie! Teleport!" He screams as cries of war explode from the army, and they charge.

I scream as the first possessed mythical attacks me. I am tackled to the ground and I squeeze my eyes shut. Then, silence. I open my eyes to find that Queen Marie was able to teleport us back to the throne room. Her eyes roll to the back of her head and she collapses into King Charles' arms. She was exhausted. I purse my lips, this was my family, I need to protect them. I don't care about the horror, I don't care about the pain, I care about my family, and I am tired of my father ruining everything!

As if reading my thoughts, my pack nods. We are going to war; together. Ethan takes my hand and tingles run through me. He holds my eyes with pain and fear etched into his expression. He sighs.I answer his fearful gaze with a smile, "We will survive, I promise." He gulps and nods, his expression changing to one of confidence, one of more pride, one of the Alpha Ethan I knew. Not this 'It's to dangerous to fight!!' one.

I look towards the pack again and nod. A whooshing sounds through as all of us transform. The sound of shrieking demons grew gradually louder as the army approached the castle. We run right outside to were the army stood, with their weapons pinpointed on us and with their smug grins of an easy victory plastered on their faces.Then they turn and march back up the hill.

I furrow my eyebrows, "Wha--?"Ethan narrows his eyes, "They are reforming and regaining energy from their walk. They will be back, tomorrow, with full force." He analyzes.

My eyes follow the army as they march back to the top of the hill where a camp site was being set up. We couldn't defeat this many.

"We need a plan," I whisper mentally.My pack agreed with me, but everyone was blank on ideas. My eyes kept darting back and forth between my pack, the castle, the army, the mountain, the demons, and the Demon King.

I've got a plan."I've got a plan!" I yip mentally, "Follow me!" I shout mentally as my pack watches me run inside with confused faces. They shrug, and run after me.------

Chapter 33- Plans with Old Pain

I pace around the meeting room. My pack watching me as my plan forms in my head.

I take a deep breath and stop my pacing. I turn towards the pack.

"Well?" Jack asks.

"Well.... We are going to start with the basics of what we know, and I will provide you with what you don't know."Léo raises his eyebrow as everyone else looks at me with confusion.

I sigh, my eyes traveling from member to member.

"Let's begin. We are the strongest pack around. However, that does not mean we cannot be harmed. As we know, our last demon attack almost got Athena killed."

Athena purses her lips.

"However, if you remember, Jack was there to save her."The group nods and I continue, "Jack, how were you able to defeat a demon? A possessy in that case?"

Jack furrows his eyebrows, "I don't remember...."

"Exactly," I confirm. "When you fight demons, if you destroy one, the final defense from the demon is removing your memory so that you don't kill more demons." I look towards Ethan, "Remember when I was fighting Pierce and Hunter in the forest after our kidnapping?"

Ethan nods, yet everyone was still confused."Well, before I had that fist fight with Hunter, I was actually fighting a demon hybrid. A human that was half demon fought me. Since it wasn't all demon, it wasn't able to completely remove my memory. Now at I saw who the demon king is, I remembered how I defeated the hybrid."

Everyone leans a little closer in."Through magic...." I whisper. Now Linda stood confused, "How with magic? You are an animal transformer!"

I respond to her, "That is true, but like Jack, I have the power to control elements. Jack destroyed the possessy demon with his water power without knowing it. I destroyed the demon with my ice power. And Ethan destroyed his own personal demon, when he was younger, with the fire."

Ethan gives a small smile as Linda blinks in understanding.Léo crosses his arms, "How about the Shadow demons? How do we destroy them?""How do you make a shadow disappear?" I pause.

"You shine a light on it." Anna and I say together. She holds my gaze, biting her lip,"Shadow demons won't die just because a light is flashed on them, what light are you talking about?"

"The light of team work..." I say quietly. It sounded corny, but it was true.It was Ethan's turn for disbelief, "Really, how does that work?" He asks, sarcasm dripping from his voice.

I sigh, "Let me start from the beginning then. You see, my mother was a animal transformer. She was the one and only Phoenix, one of the most powerful creatures for she never could die."Some looks of surprise were shot my way.

"However, every year, the phoenix needs to revive itself. It turns into a ball of flame and turns into ashes. Those ashes would eventually reform back into the phoenix. When my father learned that my mother was a phoenix, he immediately wanted to use her to get to the top of the mythical world. My mother disagreed, refusing to be used to inflict pain and fear for money and power. Daniel was furious. He told her that she was not loyal to him. The irony was he was already cheating on her with Sheila's mom. But he hid his anger well. When it was my mother's time to revive herself, she turned into her ashes. But never turned back." I felt the sting of grief reach me.

"Daniel took her ashes and scattered them around. You see, for a Phoenix to revive itself, it needed all of its ashes together. When the ashes separate, unless all are found, the Phoenix is as good as dead. However, I did not know that. All I knew was that Daniel came home with a grief sicken face and said that my mother was dead. At first, I didn't believe it. 'How could she be dead? It couldn't be true!' I was in a crazied state, running around the house opening all doors and toppling everything down to find my mother. Daniel threw me outside and told me to scram until I was normal. I ran into the forest and finally sadness hit me. Then, the anger that transformed me into my animal hit me. My memory went blank after that. But when I finally woke up, in the middle of the forest, I realized that my father had killed her....."

A single tear trailed down my cheek.My pack was looking at me with sympathy. I quickly wipe that tear away and continue.

"I lived with Daniel and his new bride for some time, before being sent to Mythical School..."My scar burned even more. I haven't put the cream on it. So my skin felt like it was on fire; and I let it. I wince as a stronger wave of pain hit me. Ethan looks at me in worry, "Your scar?"

I nod. "My scar happened in Mythical school..... The night of the escape. Screams and yells were heard as all of us were escaping. The school was on fire, the guards chasing down and tasering kids, a huge hole was in the building, and demons were running around loose, attacking everyone. I was able to escape unnoticed by the chaos that was happening around me. Everyone was fighting for their own lives. But we were being caught like sardines. It was night time and the forest was haunting. We could be caught easily in there, but also with difficulty. I remember stopping by the edge of the forest. The screams of children ringing in my ears, and I was frozen in fear...Then a smoothing hum came from my left. I was hypnotized. This hum as causing a calm feeling to settle over my bones, instead of the fear of being caught and/or killed. I walked toward the sound. I went deeper inside the forest until I ended up near a small pond. "

"Floating above the pond, was the spirit of the Phoenix, my mother. She gave me one of her smiles that I always loved and I remember trying to run to her. But she shook her head no. I stopped. Right then, lightning struck from above, hitting my back. The pain, was the feeling of burning alive. I remember collapsing on the floor and darkness taking me. I felt the cool hand on my mother caressing my cheek, before she disappeared also. I woke as soon as the feeling disappeared. The screams of pain and horror still echoed in the distance, most of the children still have not escaped. I saw an image of a Phoenix in my mind and calmness flowed through me. I had to save the other kids, even if I didn't know them. Then, my scar ex-ploded with pain. It forced my transformation on me. Once again I didn't remember what animal was, I just had one thought: together.""Then, I roared. The forest around me shook. The screams creased just slightly and soon enough the kids started coming to me. Somehow, we connected and figured out how to take out the guards and the demons. Then we attacked back....."

I paused, the packing taking in what I said."Demons are destroyed through teamwork. Every time someone charges at a shadow demon, it disappears. It reappcars bchind the person and usually destroys them. The only way to kill a shadow is through light. Right when the demon is about to disappear and reappear, a light needs to be flashed at it; a light held by someone pure. Then the demon disappears, and it stays gone forever..."

My scar burned and I grit my teeth. My pack looks at me with awe. "How did you know that?" Jack whispered. I shrugged and gave a small smile, "Experience. That and as a free-runner I ran into some demons a couple of times."

Athena sighs, "Kate, that sounds amazing, but how do we take on thousands of demons?"I grin, "The same way the kids at Mythical School took out hundreds of demons; together."

Anna rolls her eyes, "Ya, but this little gang can't take out that many!"I smirk, "I said together not alone."Anna opens her mouth to rebuke again, but the door bell rings.A butler appears in front of us. "You have guests." He says monotone and disappears.I smile at my pack as they look between themselves completely confused. My scar keeps burning.We walk towards the entrance of the castle and my scar becomes more and more painful. As we reach the door, I collapse. Ethan's warm arms catch me. "Kate!"

"I'll be fine, just open the door." I tell my nervous pack mates.Anna purses her lips and her hand grasps the golden door handle. As the door opens she gasps.Her mouth drops as she turns to me. I give a weak smile, my skin feeling like it was on fire from my scar.

"What?" Jack asks her. She opens the door completely and then the rest of the pack's mouths drop. There, on the field, stood everyone from Mythical Academy. All the packs, all looking determined and proud to stand up against the demons with us. Esmerelda and Jazzy were standing in the huge crowd, grinning broadly and everyone else we knew like Mr.Grim, Ms.Sharpfang, everyone.. Everyone was here. The hundreds of students that belonged to Mythical Academy and other pure mythicals were here. My scar called them, and my thoughts transferred to all of them.

I smile to Anna, "Together."Then darkness took me as the pain finally took me under.

Chapter 34- Final Fight

I woke from my unexpected slumber a few hours later. It was early morning and everyone was now hustling around the castle. Everyone was stern looking, had weapons, and were talking strategy or training. A whistle blew and everyone dashed for the outside, it was war time.

Now, we were all standing opposing from Daniel's demon army. Half our large army had flashlights, the other half had magic. Fairies hovered in the back. Animal transformers were in their animal forms, crouched and ready to prounce near the front. Werewolves were mixed into that mix and so were a few vampires.

The deep robotic voice of Daniel echoes through, "Not surrendering I see?""Never!" I yell back. "Well, see all of you in hell." He smirks.He removes his sword and points it at us. This time, we were ready.

"CHARGE!" Ethan screams and howls of war exploded around us. Jack, Ethan, and I transform into our mythical animals.

The demons charged at us, but we were ready. We worked fluently together. Groups of mythicals killing demon after demon. Hisses, snarls, cries of pain, screams, yells, and war cries sounded around us. My large dragon body easily knocked demons off their feet. I slam my feet in the ground, and ice explodes from under me. Demons' feet stick to the ice. They all look at me with hate until horror fills their eyes. I feel the power radiate from my gorgeous mate as he steps forward, right by my side. He opens his mouth and flames shoot out, burning all of the demons that were stuck. Anna and Léo were working perfectly together to take out shadows. Linda and Will were taking out possessys and so were Athena and Jack. I attack another demon, knocking him off of one of our mythicals. I feel Athena run up my scales. She flips off me, throwing her dagger and killing a demon up ahead.

The war kept going, killing demon after demon with more and more injuries on our side.The chaos was torturous, but exciting. Adrenaline flooded trough me, enhancing everything.My nose caught the scent of a wolf, a demon wolf and I blindly charge after the scent. I go farther and farther away from the main chaos and farther up the hill.

"I knew I would catch you little dragon." Daniel's deep voice chuckles as he steps forward from the forest. He was a wolf, a wolf the size of me, a dragon. He had pure black fur that had smoke rising from it. His eyes were blood red, and his teeth hungry for my death.

"Daniel!" I hiss and began circling him."Daughter." He muses smugly.I snarl, "I'm not your daughter!""So you have repeated." He charges, biting my back leg. I scream out in pain and lash out, kicking him with my other leg.He backs up with three scratches across his face from my claws. The wolf of Daniel growls. With a howl, he charges again.

He tackles me to the ground, my belly up and open. He lunges for my throat. I move my neck away. He lunges again, this time, I was too slow. I screech out in pain as his teeth close around my throat. My legs start kicking out, trying to hit him. I manage to scratch him, but he just growls in pain, his teeth clamping harder down on my throat. I couldn't breath. My lungs burned with the need to breath. My vision became dimmed. I couldn't die like this, I didn't even give him a fight! Then images of Ethan popped up in my mind. The smiling face of my pack and our experiences together appeared in my mind. I will not die like this!

I roar put, and with the last of my breath I ram my legs into his underbelly and cut downwards, cutting his stomach. He howls in pain, letting me go. I slam my hind legs into him, kicking him off me.

Now, both of us were panting and bleeding heavily. "So, you were the enemy that needed to know my weakness." I hiss quietly."Yes..." Daniel growls back.

I charge slamming into him with my shoulder. He flies a few feet back, slamming into a tree. His red eyes glow a little brighter with furry. He pushes off from the tree and jumps toward me. I jump out of the way but not before his teeth skim over my shoulder. I yelp in pain, jumping backward. He attacks again, grabbing my front leg. I bite his ear and he lets go, whimpering.

He has the advantage! What do I have that he doesn't?He charges and I shoot an ice flame from my mouth. It melts faster than I can blink. I couldn't use that.

"Kate? Where are you?!" Ethan shrills in fear. I block him out of my thou ghts.We keep circling each other, lunging for attack and defending back.

I notice that Daniel was staying away from my wings. He charges again and I snap open my wings, roaring and making myself look bigger. He pauses for a little, unsure whether to attack or not. Gotta love animal instincts.

I use that against him. With my wings open I attack him. He dodges just in time, and lunges at my leg. My wing beats down, slapping him. He whines, staggering back in shock.

I hiss, tensing my wings on an open position at my sides. This was my advantage. He growls, recovering from his shock and tries to attack my throat again. My wing slams into him, knocking him off of his feet and into a tree. I attack, ramming my claws into his stomach. Daniel snarls in pain, pushing me off of him. His teeth close around my wing and I roar in pain. Electricity was shooting from my wings, but it wasn't harming him. I hit him with my head, sending him flying off me.

He was weakening, and that was exciting my dragon. I growl in excitement as he has trouble standing back up. He howls back in anger. Daniel charges. My mind blanks and I was no longer in control. Everything hurt, but I couldn't feel it. My dragon body is lifted upwards by my wings. Daniel lunges by me, missing me and crashing into another tree. I zoom upwards, hovering above him. He snarls, jumping up to catch me.

I dive, dodging his teeth, but planting my own teeth into his throat. He howls in fear and pain as my teeth tighten around his throat. He knew that was his fatal mistake. I fly us higher and higher, the wolf of Daniel trying to scratch me in fear. But I wasn't feeling emotions, I was just a war machine; destroying the head of the snake. My wings shut against my sides and we plummet down to earth. I release him from my teeth and use my head to push him faster to the upcoming ground. He tries to fight me or catch onto my scales, but I was dodging him. Finally, as the ground got even closer, my wings shot open, lifting me back up into the sky. Daniel howls in fear, realizing what I did. I watches as his figure came closer and closer to the ground. I squeeze my eyes shut as the Demon King reached the ground. A bone chilling 'CRUNCH' sounded through the air and I grit my teeth as he reached the destination.

I open my eyes to find the dead body of Daniel, the Demon King on the group, with blood everywhere. A dark whispy thing floats up from the body. It was the demon that possessed Daniel. It looks up to me and nods its head in respect. Then, it dives down, disappearing into the ground.

The war cries in the distance crease. The sound of confusion takes hold instead. I tilt my wings, still numb. I fly toward the many fighters back on the main area and land down. The scattered bodies of possessed mythicals lay like broken robots. The pure mythicals look around in confusion, looking up to me.

Ethan runs up to me in worry and nuzzles me with his dragon head. I nudge him back and hold his eyes, opening up my thoughts. His eyes widen and he smiles. Then, he roars in victory. All of the mythicals join; all roaring and yelling their hearts out from joy. The war has been won. I look around and realize that without each of these mythicals fighting these demons, I would have never been able to take out Daniel, his demon minions would have helped him. Each of us did our part, even if it wasn't finishing the deal. I was still numb, so the thought was heart warming.

I transform back and Ethan follows me. He runs up to me, grabbing me in his arms. He laughs, hugging me tightly, "You did runner!" Then, I break. I cry and laugh into him, clutching onto him as if he was my life source. He kisses my forehead and whispers, "I love you." Then he scolds, "Don't ever do that again!"

I giggle slightly, my tears drying, "I love you too...." I smile. The pack runs up to me, all of them had tears in their eyes. "We did it. " Anna cries, a full blow smile on her face. "I nod my head, "We did do it...." I take Ethan's hand and smile up to him, "Together."

--------Hey guys! This was the last chapter! I would love it if you could tell me what you think. Being this is my first story, I would love feedback. There is just the epilogue and Mythical Academy is done. Also, if you can check out my next and newest story: Alpha's Princess, I would greatly appreciate it! Its got the same mythical flow as this story, but a little more fighting and kicking butt!

Here is a preview:

Once upon a time, there lived a poor little girl in the dirty streets of the human world. With her parents gone and her having to survive alone, she became strong and stiff. As the little girl grew older, she learned dark secret of heart-break, forever sealing her heart in a wall of steel. From that day forward she decided never to want to love again. With her heart set, she became one of the best thieves around, cold-hearted and smart. She went by the code name "Nightstrike". Nobody knew who this thief was, or how to stop them. She was as fast as lightning and left without a trace when morning came. However, one day she was finally caged.

Her jail was those crystal green eyes and light blonde hair. With one flash of that dazzling smile she bowed down, her steel heart broken by the man. The man was captivated by this poor little thief and his heart fell for her.The two ran off together, never wanting to stop staring into each other's love struck eyes, and not caring about the world. The girl forever knew that he was only hers and he knew that she was only his. Then they lived happily ever after.

Except, that's not how the story went. That 'happily ever after' never happened. Actually, everything in the last two paragraphs never happened.

My name is Syrina. I am NightStrike and I have entered the largest pack in the world.

My cousin, my mortal enemy. My heart, stone. But my fighting spirit, burning with desire.

With the brink of war of rogues and power-hungry men versus pure and powerful mythicals, my story has just begun. And my knives, have yet to strike...

Epilogue

W ell, Mythical Academy has finally come to an end. I highly doubt that I will make a book two. To tell you the truth, I am so amazed by the amount of people who actually read this book, and to all the readers: Thank you so much! It meant so much to me to know my own world can be given to some of you amazing people.

Again, thank you. But if you like.... My newest story is up and I would greatly appreciate it if you could check it out. It is called Alpha's Princess. Its got the same mythical flow as this story, but a little more fighting and kicking butt!

Here is a preview:

Once upon a time, there lived a poor little girl in the dirty streets of the human world. With her parents gone and her having to survive alone, she became strong and stiff. As the little girl grew older, she learned dark secret of heart-break, forever sealing her heart in a wall of steel. From that day forward she decided never to want to love again. With her heart set, she became one of the best thieves around, cold-hearted and smart. She went by the code name "Nightstrike". Nobody knew who this thief was, or how to stop them. She was as fast as lightning and left without a trace when morning came. However, one day she was finally caged.

Her jail was those crystal green eyes and light blonde hair. With one flash of that dazzling smile she bowed down, her steel heart broken by the man. The man was captivated by this poor little thief and his heart fell for her.The two ran off together, never wanting to stop staring into each other's love struck eyes, and not caring about the world. The girl forever knew that he was only hers and he knew that she was only his. Then they lived happily ever after.

Except, that's not how the story went. That 'happily ever after' never happened. Actually, everything in the last two paragraphs never happened.

My name is Syrina. I am NightStrike and I have entered the largest pack in the world.

My cousin, my mortal enemy. My heart, stone. But my fighting spirit, burning with desire.

With the brink of war of rogues and power-hungry men versus pure and powerful mythicals, my story has just begun. And my knives, have yet to strike...

"Daddy! Daddy! Daddy! Mommy! Mommy! Mommy!" A little bundle of job hops around our bed.

Ethan sighs with happiness, still holding me around my waist. He nuzzles his face into my neck, sighing with happiness. It's been six years since the war. The wedding was the month right after the war. Life has never been better.

"Hey Princess, it's New Years morning," he whispers huskily into my ear before kissing the bite on my neck that claimed me as his. I smile slightly, my eyes still closed.

"I know love. The little product of our love jumping on my legs told me so." Yesterday's party was really crazy, and we were still asleep. Everyone from the mythical kingdom, our kingdom, came to the castle to party. Afterwards, we all went home. We were the last ones for we had to clean up, then we went pack to the pack house.

I feel something squirm between Ethan's and my body. My eyes open and I flip around to find my beautiful four year old daughter, Catelyn, looking at me with bright blue eyes. "Good morning mommy!" She giggles. I pull her into me, hugging her tightly and kissing the top of her dark brown hair. "Good morning angel." I whisper. She snuggles into me before looking up at me, "We get to open presents this morning right?" I smile. "That's right love, that is if daddy lets us." Catelyn turns, looking towards Ethan, "Can we open the presents daddy?" She asks so innocently. Ethan was now propelled up on his elbow. He purses his lips, "Hmm.... Let me think about it."

I smile, "Oh come on honey, let her open it."Ethan pouts at me, "But she didn't give me a good morning hug."I laugh as Catelyn's eyes widen and she tackles Ethan into a hug. "I'm sorry daddy! Please forgive me!" She rushes and gives him a kiss on the cheek. Ethan chuckles, "it's alright kitten." He hugs her tightly before ruffling her hair. "You can go open presents."

"Yay!" She jumps out of the queen sized bed and rushes to the door. She stops before she gets there. "Mommy, will Matthew open presents too?""Happy New Years baby." Ethan whispers to me and kisses me on the lips before shuffling out of bed.

I also get out of bed before answering, "Yes honey, Matthew has his own presents.""Cool!" Catelyn answers. "Can I go wake Aunt Linda, and Uncle

William?"Ethan chuckles and quickly slips on some pants and slips on a shirt. "Sure Princess, go ahead."Catelyn squeals and I smile as I put on some jeans and a sweater. "Ooo! How about Aunt Anna and Uncle Léo?" She asks with innocents.This time I laugh, "How about later. Alex and Simon gave them a hard time last night. You can go wake up Grandma Marie and Grandpa Charles." Yes, King Charles and Queen Marie gave up their kingdom to Ethan and I once we married.

Catelyn squeals again, "Okay! Bye mommy! Bye daddy! See you soon!" She dashes out the door and I laugh.Ethan creeps behind me. Ethan and I both have changed. We took over the Mythical kingdom with our pack, Ethan started to had slight stubble across his jawline, and I decided to grow my hair out longer and be not as harsh. He became wiser and many say he was one of the best rulers that the land has seen. We rarely ever have to use our dragons for problems in the kingdom. Which is good, though rogues were still a problem, and sometimes Pierce is too. Luckily, Catelyn will be able to transform soon and we need to be there when that happens.

His arms wrap around my torso and pull me into his body."Happy New Years sweetheart." He smirks, kissing me on the cheek.I smile back and turn around, still in his arms. "Happy New Years blood-sucker." I kiss him on the lips.

Crying starts up in the corner of our room as we break the kiss. I smile, "I got it."I walk towards the crib, picking up Mathew, our one and a half year old son. He stops crying when I pick him up and yawns, showing his baby fangs as they have started to grow.

"Good morning sunshine." I smile, holding him up. Ethan comes up and takes him from my hands, "Hey there big guy! Look at you! Your first New Years and you survived!" Mathew giggles slightly. Mathew also had his father's eyes and hair, but his features were mine. Catelyn's features were also mine. Though both were vampires.

I take Mathew from his father's hands. I kiss Ethan again, "Come on, everyone will be up soon."

**

Everyone was seated in the living room. Catelyn was by the tree looking for presents with her name on it. Will was cuddling with tired Linda. She was pregnant now for eight months with a boy. Athena and Jack and were cuddled together on another couch. They got married a year ago, and just came back from their six-month honeymoon. Anna and Léo were cuddled together on a third couch, with their two twin one-year-old boys, Simon and Alex, sitting happily and chewing on their fingers.

I sat with Ethan on the other couch, him cuddling with me and with his hand on my belly and his other hand holding laughing Mathew who was playing with his new toy. Yes, I was three months pregnant with another girl.

He kisses my ear making me shiver. "It's sad Catelyn and Mathew couldn't have another New Year's present." I roll my eyes, "I wasn't in the mood, after just having William, wanting another baby was difficult. Be happy you get this baby girl in five months!"

Ethan smiles and kisses me, "I know love. I am excited for our little girl and boy to have a sister,"I sigh and lean back against Ethan, "Three months pregnant, gave birth a year ago, and have a four year old running around. How are we surviving?" I ask.

Ethan kisses the top of my head, "We are surviving with happiness."I smile in agreement.Catelyn rips open her present and gasps. It was another toy horse. But she loves them. She hugs the toy tightly before running over to Marie and Charles and giving them a big hug. "Thank you grandpa and grandma!" Marie kisses Catelyn's head as Charles hugs her, "Your welcome deary."

The door to the pack house bursts open and a frizzy-hair witch glides in. "HoHoHo! Merry New Years!" The pack laughs as Catelyn's eyes go wide. "Grandma Esmerelda!" She runs up to Esmerelda and gives her a hug before starting at the bag that was floating next to her. "Are those presents?" She squeaks.

I chuckle and Ethan smiles. "Why yes! And some are even for you!" Esmerelda smiles while Catelyn squeals. Esmerelda then joins us in the living room. She drops the bag off at the Christmas tree and instantly Catelyn is digging through. "Oh my gosh! More presents!" She squeals, her voice muffled as she digs into the bag. My pack laughs.

Ethan sighs, "You know darling, we have got ourselves a pretty good famil y." I sigh, completely relaxed in Ethan's arms. I take Mathew from him and put him in my own lap. My eyes scan the living room. Everyone was happy, laughing, joyful, and full of love.

I nod my head, "We have an amazing family and we will keep it that way; no matter how bumps the road are in the future. Together we will stand."

The end.